For Charles and Daniel

ACKNOWLEDGEMENTS

Some of these stories have previously been published in *Scotland on Sunday, Edinburgh Review, Cutting Teeth, Flamingo Scottish Short Stories, Full Strength Angels (NWS)* and *Chapman.*

'Beyond Vigilance' and 'Flowers of the Moon' were broadcast on BBC Radio 4.

The author would like to thank the sponsors of the Robert Louis Stevenson Memorial Award: Christian Salvesen plc, the National Library of Scotland and the Scottish Arts Council, for her fellowship in Grez-sur-Loing, without which this book would have taken much longer to complete.

ACKNOWLEDGEMENTS

Some of these stories have previously been published in [illegible] Scottish [illegible] [illegible] [illegible] [illegible] [illegible] [illegible] and [illegible].

[illegible] and [illegible] the Moon were broadcast on BBC Radio.

The author would like to thank the trustees of the Robert Louis Stevenson Memorial Award, [illegible], the National Library of Scotland and the Scottish Arts Council [illegible] without whom this book would have taken much longer to complete.

CONTENTS

Swan Lake

I HAVE A memory from a long time ago but so clear, every little detail. France in springtime, early spring when the world was just coming to after the winter. There were violets everywhere pushing through the dewy grass, their petals uncurling shyly, opening up little by little. A grey, still morning, birds everywhere; on the ground and the water, in the trees and the sky. I've never seen so many birds; finches and woodpeckers and doves and many I didn't know. The trees were completely still, the new catkins drooping like little monkey tails and fat, green-tipped buds thrusting and glistening stickily and making me think of sex, that luxury denied to many of us itinerants. The domiciled world finds it objectionable enough to see us eating, drinking and sleeping on the streets but sex – the homeless fornicating in public? I don't think so.

An old steam engine stood on a narrow track – TACOT DES LACS – as advertised on a rusty sign which might have dated from last century, idling there until Easter when day trippers from Paris would come and pay to be chugged round the water.

So early in the morning, the mist still drifting over the water like breath. Away from the road and its disappointments, there was no one around. One lake led on to another, each glimmering its own grey tones, drawing me away from my destination, away from the chance of a lift, though after walking all night a lift had begun to seem like a very remote possibility. The long silky fingers of the lakes beckoned and it was easy to imagine a sprite in the mist, luring tired, hungry people deeper and deeper into the forest until they were lost. But that's not the way it was; that was tiredness playing tricks on me. I found out later that the path formed a long loop round the lakes which eventually led back to the same spot.

It was not because I was drunk that I had that idea. I don't drink. Many of us do but not me. I don't swear either, unless I am very angry, and then only under my breath; I never ever shout. For some people shouting is a liberating thing, a way of getting things out, spring-cleaning their heads and starting afresh but for me, the sound of shouting . . . no, I don't like the sound of shouting.

There was no human noise at all except the crunch of my own feet on the path, my own stomach growling for food, my own breathing heavy and hard as if my chest were full of lead. I found an empty cartridge on the path, a little steel-grey plastic rocket, and picked it up, I don't know why, maybe just for something to hold. The woods turned out to be a game reserve. It happens everywhere; you see somewhere which from a distance looks free and welcoming but when you get closer there's barbed wire or an electric fence or a wall with broken glass along the top. And signs, of course. RÉSERVE DE CHASSE in this case. With a gun or a fishing rod – and a permit, mind – there would be plenty food to be had. But I had stopped thinking about food; the thought of eating a bird or a fish was not in my mind at all. I was too caught up with watching the swans. There were other birds on the lake too, little black moorhens puttering about, geese and ducks all making ripples on the calm water but it was the swans I remember most vividly, gliding across the water so poised, clean and white, swivelling their dangerously beautiful heads.

Some were feeding too, backsides exposed to the sky, fluttering like flowers. And being spring the mating season was on the go. On the trees the ladybirds were stotting about, stuck together, bum to bum. Odd just to continue going about your travels while having sex, but maybe they're a tribe of itinerants and if they stop too long, some other kind of insect will want to know why.

The swans: they seemed to be moving around at random, ripples fanning out behind them. One of the males had begun to pursue a female, casually at first but determinedly skimming along behind her. It's easy to see why dancers try to imitate swans, all that stylish swishing. But isn't it always the males who do the showing off, fluffing themselves up, coiling their necks back and tucking their heads into their feathers. More like fan dancers than ballerinas, really. It was a subtle, casual pursuit, the male showing off, the female swimming on apparently unconcerned but keeping her distance all the same. And then the male rising out of the water, huge and heavy and slow, wings creaking, neck straight as an oar, flying barely a hand's breadth above the water, the female continuing, playing hard to get.

It's the swans I remember most, and the shy violets, and another all too familiar sign: STATIONNEMENT INTERDIT AUX NOMADES. Sounds less harsh in French but the message is the same in any language: keep on walking, mate, don't stop here, take your carcass someplace else. I can't remember how I got to where I was going or even why I was in France in the first place. There must have been a reason but . . . when you move around so much the road becomes not so much a route from one place to another as a place in itself and moving along it is just part of survival, like breathing. One thread of tarmac leads to another, they are all part of the same loop. The places on the way only matter to those who live in them or come to visit and compare their lives to others in the domiciled world. It was the same that day, nothing has changed other than the place, the time and my method . . .

Then it was water but the thought of fouling up the lake, of distressing the birds put me off. As well as the violets I remember another plant which, unless my nose was deceiving me, smelled a bit like piss. Anyway, it reminded me of a good few stairways and closemouths; the perfume of the streets . . .

Here, the city streets are stuffed to the gills with visitors and the police have been doing their annual clean-up so the tourists' views aren't ruined by too many of us lying around, living our distasteful, disturbing lives in public. One year somebody made a show about us, put some of our more colourful characters on the stage. It was very popular and even won a prize. People laughed and cried and clapped like hell at the end. A full house every night, television interviews, photographers and a good tap for some. It's one thing for tourists to pay money to see us on the stage, another to trip over us on the street.

RÉSERVE DE CHASSE. Hunters don't mess about. They see something moving and contrive to stop it moving. Maybe that's what gave me the idea but it didn't fucking work and I'm angry which is why I'm swearing, angry for failing yet again.

It's so clear. I keep thinking there must be something else about it which is important. Just the flat grey water, the swans, the violets. I had stopped at the woods to get away from the road where nobody'd picked me up all night. Not the first time that had happened; walking at night was something I knew pretty damn well. On quiet roads it wasn't too bad; just the headlights to contend with, the weather and the lack of decent footwear. The usual. Where I was coming from or going to who knows, it was quite likely that I was just keeping on the move because it's safer not to stop anywhere too long. I can't think why I was in France. I don't know anyone in France. It was probably just something about the place, the way one memory leads to another like the lakes, on and on and then, without warning, you find you're back at the beginning again, neither lost nor found.

The swans: they mate for life. But how do they choose their partners; by the way breast feathers fold into each other like heavenly pillows, the quality of their dry rattling calls, or the sight of another's backside waving in the air, an unearthly feather flower? And once they've chosen a mate, are they happy? Is spending your life gliding across the lake more bearable when you've a partner to share the moving around with? Not France, or Germany. Spain, of course it was Spain. Was her name really Violetta, or is that just me making things up again? Violetta and the cheese – a wedge of pale, moon-coloured cheese, creamy like her arms, Violetta talking to me and never for a moment looking away, making me listen to words I couldn't understand, holding me with her eyes. Violetta, the cold winter sun on her hands as she sliced the cheese.

Spain, down on the south coast somewhere. Africa

across the water. I didn't go to Africa. You can't walk to Africa. I did ask. I did go down to the docks and see if there was anything doing on the boats but there were plenty other needy people who could understand orders and curses, so fair's fair, nothing doing. Sitting on the sea wall, the breeze ruffling her hair. I asked her where I could buy some food. She took one long steady look at me, cut off a slice of her cheese and handed it over, talking talking talking, God knows what she was saying, I just stood there chewing and nodding and wanting to squeeze my thanks into her . . . but instead, when I'd finished eating, I shook her hand, turned away and in on myself once more.

Maybe her name wasn't Violetta and the connection with the lakes is something else altogether. Violets. African violets. Oh yes. African violets. All wrapped up nicely in shiny cellophane, a little card with a picture of the flowers I'd bought, a printed LOVE FROM . . . and my name crushed alongside in my best seven-year-old handwriting. Thanks son, she said, but violets are useless, too fragile for this climate. Just keel over and die if you turn your back on them for a moment.

Warm, too warm in here. I'm used to the cold more than heat. But the bed is good; a little pillow with a disposable paper cover, a clean crisp sheet and a rubber mat underneath for any mess. I've made plenty mess already. The lovely Indian woman with a long plait, gold-rimmed glasses and shy violet lips like those little flowers in France, has gone to get help. To have a woman like that touching me, to have any woman touching me now . . . God, I must smell a bit too.

It was the lakes and the swans, the thought of someone

shooting a swan. I don't know, I just thought that a crossbow would at least do the job properly, and maybe also that there was some point to it, some significance – the hunter and hunted in one – I don't know. The bow was too heavy, I was weak, my hands shook like a drunk's . . .

My mother thought the violets were too fragile to survive the harsh, inhospitable climate so she didn't want them, didn't want to be bothered with a plant which hadn't the will to live, she'd had enough of things keeling over. Maybe if she'd just tried to like my present a little it would have opened its heart-shaped petals and stood up straight and brave.

And me, even if I was too shy and too quiet, curling into myself, turning my head away and stopping up my ears. It was not my mother, I kept telling myself, it wasn't her, it was just a noise which would pass over like a plane and everything would be all right again. But soon the plane didn't pass over, it began crashing around inside the house, the room, my own head, crashing and exploding. One day somebody from the social came and dug me out of the wreckage.

The lovely Indian woman has returned, with help. She tells me I look like a saint in a painting she saw in Florence, from the Renaissance. The steel arrowhead burns my chest, my blood blooms on the white sheet . . . Did I see a wounded swan crawling to its nest, wings torn and bloody? Did I hear a shot? No help for the bird, no knives or needles . . . nothing for the pain. I'm so lucky.

She is above me, looking down, her eyes deep and dark behind her glasses. She is holding my wrist and telling me to count backwards from a hundred. Her hand is small and warm like a little bird. She is smiling and looking at her watch. *Africa is across the water. Grey shawls of mist wrapped around the thin limbs of the trees. The flowers too fragile, not worth the bother. Violetta cutting cheese on her open palm. The cheese smooth against my dry, swollen tongue . . .*

I turn away and into myself, and my own white-hot ecstasy . . .

Handholds

SUMMER DUSK. THREE teenage girls, in silhouette, tilt backwards, bracing themselves against the steep slope of the hill. Laughing, they link arms, sway and stagger from side to side, kicking up their legs in a ragged chorus line. Above them, a flicker of late birds or early bats, a spatter of stars. Below, a single pale wave licks the shore. In the hills, the distant waterfall appears to flow upward, to grasp at the cliff like a huge silver hand. The evening smells of sun-dried seaweed, heather.

Where they are is barely a village; a spill of cottages clings to the curving bay, at the bend in the road a red, unvandalised telephone box is waist-deep in thistles and the shoreside campsite holds a solitary, unoccupied caravan. The single-track road whips around the fretted coastline, a wild reel of hairpin bends, rockfalls and sheer, deadly drops. In the distance, the headlights of a car wink and vanish, wink and vanish.

—It's nice here, says Sarah, but . . .

—But borin, says Dianne.

Dianne sighs loudly and chews a strand of her long, straight hair.

—Ah wish Glen wis drivin that car. Ah wish Glen was beltin roon they bends tae meet me, says Dianne.

—Has Glen got a car?

—Nuh.

—Still. At least you can wish aboot somebody real, says Sarah.

—Ah miss him, says Dianne.

—It's only been four days.

—Ken. Feels like for ever.

—Fuck off, says Sarah. Ye're makin me jealous. Ah've naebody tae miss. God, mibbe ah'll never huv naebody tae miss.

Above their heads the sky is inky. At the horizon, it's pink with thin mint-green lozenges of cloud.

—See they clouds, says Sarah. Ah fancy jeans that colour.

—God, says Dianne. Make yer arse look massive, a colour like that.

—Ken, says Sarah. But ah'd get noticed.

The third girl, Ciara, breaks the line, waves her arms above her head and jiggles her hips until she stumbles and falls face down on the hill, laughing helplessly.

—Nae mair Hooch for her, says Dianne. You hear me, Ciara, NAE MAIR HOOCH! Ye're pissed awready.

—OOOOHH!

—Ye can hear that all right, can ye no?

Ciara rubs her bluish, moonlit cheeks against the hillside, trying out the feel of grass, moss and heather. Her head feels hot, bubbly and everything is funny, everything; the grass tickling her face, Dianne and Sarah shaking their heads at her, the car bobbing along on the coast road.

—Are we goin doon the beach, then? says Dianne.

—Well, we could try the Pizza Hut first, or the chippie. Or one of aw they discos doon the road, says Sarah. Or we could just eye up the talent on the streets.

—Fuck off, says Dianne.

—CAAAA, says Ciara.

—Aye, says Sarah. Car. Dianne wishes Glen wis in it.

—GEHHH?

—Get up ye deef bugger and come oan.

Like a traffic policeman, Sarah beckons to Ciara who stumbles obediently to her feet. The three girls walk, skip and stagger down the hill until they reach the short stretch of road which leads through the caravan site to the beach. A couple of munching sheep scutter in front of the girls, unable to decide what to do next.

—Stupit things, says Dianne.

—Pea brains, says Sarah.

—ShhhhEEEE, says Ciara.

She stretches out a hand to stroke one of their silly, bony noses but the sheep back off nervously; one of them slips into the ditch. Ciara laughs but she's sorry that the sheep don't trust her. She'd never hurt an animal. She loves animals, their warm, comforting smells, their uncomplicated eyes.

As they pass the empty caravan, Ciara stops, presses her face against the window. There's not much to see but the glass is cool against her skin and when she steps back, her mouth leaves a kiss mark. With a finger, she draws two mismatched eyes above the smudged impression of her mouth.

Dianne and Sarah race each other to the shore, trainers thudding softly and throwing up arcs of fine sand. Clownlike, Ciara follows, arms and legs flying out in all directions. When she reaches the water's edge, she birls round and round.

—Get back, says Sarah. Ye'll fa doon daein that. Ye'll get soaked and us two'll get the blame for it.

—Ye're wastin yer breath, says Dianne. She hastae see yer mooth. And ye huvtae say everythin dead slow.

—Ken, says Sarah. Ken. Ah've kent her as long as you, Dianne. But she willny look at ma mooth, will she? She willny fuckin stand still.

Dizzy, Ciara veers into the water; Sarah grabs her and pulls her back. Ciara's head jerks backwards and a thin harsh cry, like a gull's, flies from her mouth as she twists free from Sarah's grasp and hits out, a frenzy of elbows, fists, knees. Sarah gasps and groans, doubles up and clutches at her stomach.

—Fucksake, Ciara!

—Ye ken us, Ciara! Sarah roars. Ye've kent us since ye were wee. It's deep, the water. And ye cannae swim.

Sarah slowly straightens up, wipes the sand from her jeans.

—Ah'm sair all over.

The small waves make a secretive, whispering sound. Ciara clomps off along the shore, hugging herself. Nothing's funny any more, nothing's a laugh, it's all gone dark and cold. Dianne and Sarah watch as, at the far end of the beach, Ciara disappears behind a jagged stack of rock.

—The rocks here are really really old, says Dianne. Millions and millions of years old. Folk say they're the oldest rocks in the world.

—Huv ye finished yir geography project, then? says Sarah.

—No yet, but there's tons of leaflets in the cottage. Ye widnae think there'd be much tae write aboot a wee place like this but there's stacksa stuff. Aboot rocks and deid folk, ken.

—But nae much need for an entertainments guide. *For visitors to the area, there are nice walks and nice walks. And if ye dinnae go in for walkin, fuck off.*

—That car cannae be far away now. Ah can hear it.

—So can ah.

Dianne and Sarah look up at the road expectantly.

Ciara begins to clamber up the smooth black rocks, still warm from the day's sun, warm as a body. Her hands feel for holds. In the hairline crevices, crisp, salty weed and striped cockles crackle beneath her fingers. She pulls a cockle loose with her nail and lets it roll on to her palm. In her ear, her inner ear, as the doctor explained, pointing to the chart – there's a clever wee cockly thing, the cochlea; inside the cochlea, fluid swishes about like the sea in a shell, and the hearing hairs – all twenty thousand of them – send messages to the brain. Since she was wee and had the fever which made her eyes burn and zapped so many of those hearing hairs, she's seen the doctor's ear chart so many times she could draw it from memory.

With one ear flat against the rock, she can hear the scrape of her fingernails as she feels her way upwards. The sound is very faint, as far away as the stars but she can hear it all the same and that's what matters. She's alone with sea, rock and sky; safe, though she must be careful. Her trainers are wet, her legs long and thin, too thin. Her mum's been worrying about her and since they've been here, she's been baking cakes; every day's been like a birthday. And before the holiday, they went shopping three days in a row and her mum bought her piles of new stuff, just like Dianne and Sarah's, exactly the same.

—Must be dead cosy in a caravan, says Dianne. Wouldnae like it on ma ain, ken, but if Glen wis here . . . if he had a phone ah could phone him.

—But he doesny huv a phone. Or a car. Or a job.

—Ken.

—Ye'll just huvtae enjoy missin him. Lie doon in yer bed at night and pretend he's yer pillow or somethin. That's whit ah dae, says Sarah.

—Eh?

—Pretend.

Ciara pulls herself on to a ledge where she can dangle her legs over the edge and look down. A clear patch of violet water swarms with flashing green strands, like seaweed but too fast, too muscular; not seaweed but baby eels, pretty now, like little neon ribbons but she imagines all those babies stretching and swelling, filling up the water. Her mouth is dry. It doesn't make sense that drinking loads of Hooch makes you thirsty. Sliding back from the ledge, Ciara looks up at the sky, at the stars. She likes stars, the way they breathe out light and throw their shining rays across millions of miles of nothing. Sometimes they don't seem so far away . . .

She has climbed higher than she intended to. It's as far back down to the shore now as it is up to the road, where the approaching car dazzles her with its headlights. Ciara blinks and shrinks back on to the ledge, out of sight. The car slows down, turns in through a gap in the dyke and draws up outside the caravan. A man and a woman get out, stretch their dark, bulky bodies and stride around aimlessly, as if they're stiff from being in the car too long, then the woman hooks her arm on to the man's and they stroll to the edge of the grass where they stop and stare in the way people only do at the seaside; feet apart, bodies slack, eyes steady. They stand and stare and do nothing, watching lilac become purple, orange become red. When the woman begins to wave her free arm in front of her face, they turn and make their way back to the caravan. Midges. When the sun goes down, midges blow about the beach in loose, nipping clouds but up on the rocks where Ciara is crouching invisibly, she only has bloated flies and creepy crawlies to contend with.

The man moves from the shoulders; Ciara sees her dad in the thrusting shoulders, the jutting, angry chin. Her dad and Horse. Horse walks just like her dad, though she's never thought about it before. She doesn't ever want to see Horse again but when school starts, he'll be there, day after day, his jutting angry chin, his yellow teeth and scraped-looking skin . . . She'd like to see her dad, if only he didn't get so cross with her. Last time it was her table manners. She was eating her tea with him and he sat and watched her, his face going dark and stormy, then he wrote in big, angry letters:

YOU SOUND LIKE A PIG.
IT MAKES ME SICK.

The noise she was making was a noise she couldn't hear.

On the beach, Dianne and Sarah are pretending to talk to each other but they're not really concentrating on what they're saying; they're watching the couple in the caravan. Ciara can tell by the way their heads flick back and forth. Sometimes, too, they look over at the rocks but they can't see her; they're looking at the wrong place, at a route she might have taken, but didn't.

A yellow brick of light glows in the window of the caravan. The man bends into the boot of the car, pulls out bags and boxes and dumps them on the caravan step; the woman takes them inside. They move quickly and smoothly, without looking at each other, as if this fetching and carrying is a natural routine. And when the door of the caravan is closed, the curtain drawn, the man and woman pass back and forth, flat grey shadows, sometimes one at a time, sometimes doubling up, sliding across each other, darkening at the overlap like layers of tissue.

On the far side of the bay, her mum is in the holiday cottage, drinking wine with Dianne and Sarah's mum, enjoying the sunset and the peace and quiet, not wanting to think about what might happen when school starts again. Ciara doesn't want to think about school either. What's here now is fine, just fine. Her best friends are along the beach, stick figures on the dark sand. Maybe they're wondering where she is hiding and whether they should go and look for her. The sea is swallowing the last dregs of sunlight. Ciara is on a narrow ledge halfway up a stack, searching for handholds; in her head she can hear a deep, deep booming.

The Dead Woman and the Lover

WE'VE BEEN IN the morgue all afternoon and I'm chilled to the bone but at least – as Nick the cameraman has reminded me more than once – I can go home at the end of the night. Nick has also promised that even though I spent most of the time lying stark naked on a slab, it will all be all right in the end. In other words, any accidental flashes of pubic hair will be edited out. I tried keeping my knickers on – a hand-on-thigh shot was all that was needed – but no matter where Nick put his nimble, busy self, a white, elasticated leg band kept creeping into the frame. There was nothing for it but to bare all, shut my eyes and try to think about something other than the fact that a roomful of completely clothed people was focusing on me.

As well as being minus my clothes, I have a new, short haircut – for the likeness – which exaggerates the sharpness of my chin and cheekbones. Under the merciless lighting, I expect to look hard and haggard as well as dead but what bothers me more is the business of playing, not a character, but a real, recently living person. I've been in a number of historical dramas, breathed some life into loyal or scheming ladies' maids, feckless or streetwise waifs, a queen or two, numerous lady pioneers, witches, mistresses, molls and ruinations of famous men.

When someone has been long dead and the details of a life have gone largely unrecorded, my roles have involved more interpretation than imitation. Fictional characters, of course, provide even more scope for input on my part. But no matter how convincingly I might appear to step into another's shoes, acting is a job; I like it but also like to leave it behind. Fraser jokes about bringing Lady Macbeth home one night and Ophelia the next, though I've never played either and I'm too old now to be offered Ophelia.

Occasionally, though, a character will follow me out of the studio or off the set and lurk around the flat, popping up at inconvenient moments like an uninvited guest and snarling up the domestic routine I try to maintain, in spite of unsociable working hours and a man who has enough order at work not to need it at home. But usually when I've cleaned off my make-up and put on my own clothes again, it doesn't take too long to switch back to myself. Today, I don't know; it's the first time I've played a corpse in the reconstruction of an inquest.

Philip's project is a long shot. The facts point to suicide but gut feeling is that even if the husband didn't do the deed, he was guilty, one way or another, of causing his wife's death. A jury is not asked to make a decision on the moral question, only on the actual cause of death. The law may have been upheld but justice – we're all with the sister on this – has not prevailed. If Philip's film succeeds in drawing enough public attention to the dead woman, the case may be reopened, the truth may be revealed. If, if, if.

The dead woman had nothing noteworthy about her except her death and even that, first time round, only merited a couple of column inches. If it hadn't been for her older sister's almost lunatic persistence, the case would have been laid to rest with the minimum of fuss and interest. After all, the husband had an alibi and the suicide note was verified as genuine. But the sister insisted that there was more to it, that something had been missed. On she went, badgering anyone and everyone to consider more than the facts, to look further back than the empty vodka bottle and the cold bathwater to uncover the real cause of death. Which is why, today, I've been earning union rates by taking off my clothes for the camera.

It's been a long day; we're all tired, hungry and cold but nobody is complaining much; even Nick has kept his moans to a minimum. At his suggestion, Fraser, Philip and I have called into a nearby pub with him, a Polish place he recommended, for schnapps and blinis to take the edge off the day. Normally I'd go straight home with Fraser but the warmth and bustle of the cluttered little pub, its odours of cigars and pickled cabbage, are comforting. Nick managed to grab a table near the imitation log fire over which I'm slowly defrosting my fingers. The schnapps, served in dinky, medicinal-looking shot glasses, is having the same effect on my insides.

Fraser doesn't like my haircut; he prefers women to look soft and yielding. Ever since he arrived at the morgue, he's been quizzing me about my day, the nudity in particular. Was it essential for the purpose of reconstructing the case or just a gratuitous ogle for the crew? It can't be easy imagining your partner's body on view to millions, even if all it's doing is lying on a slab and trying not to shiver. But what's done is done; the day needs to be put to bed. I pull Philip into the conversation with Fraser as a way of slipping out of it.

I've worked with Philip before; as a director, I trust him. He's patient but thorough. As a person, he's an airy individual, who floats in and out of my life like a feather. Fraser doesn't trust Philip but Fraser doesn't trust anyone, not even himself – as he's fond of saying.

I sip my schnapps and rub the numbness out of my hands. Very much a man's pub, Nick's choice: dark wood, tobacco-stained walls plastered with photos of sporting personalities and greasy old portraits of patriarchs on horseback. The polished gantry is stocked with a wide range of vodka and schnapps. A few solo men perch on stools, nursing their drinks, and one of them, I'm convinced, is Q. We almost met a couple of years ago, at an awards ceremony. We had been seated at neighbouring tables. Neither of us won anything that night but during the envy-laden applause for those who did, we exchanged small, consolatory smiles. It's him, no doubt about it. He's been on the cover of every women's magazine this last year. Leaning against the bar, collar pulled up around his ears he looks as though he too has been in the morgue all afternoon. Either that or he's trying to avoid recognition. Getting on a bit, now, but the careworn look is part of Q's appeal to the countless women who attend cinemas to feast on his narrow, glinting eyes, his squint smile. The film doesn't matter much.

Q, aka the Lover, is running a hand along the smooth surface of the bar and I find myself following the movement of his fingers as if there were nothing else to look at in the room. This is what he does, what he's become famous for doing. Give him the part of a stubble-chinned ne'er-do-well, or clean-shaven, sensitive soul, it makes little difference to his fans. What they see is his hand caressing a table, running a fingernail along the grain of the wood. Q can – and does – make a block of wood look cherished. When he wipes his boots on a mat, sinks into an armchair, opens the latch of a window, women long to be that doormat, armchair or window latch.

On screen Q has, of course, fondled other items. He's unhooked basques and bodices, raised petticoats, slid hands beneath ballgowns and miniskirts. He has sighed and moaned, closed his eyes or kept them open in rosy, backlit interiors and grainy back alleys but it's not for the sex scenes themselves that women flock to the Roxy, the Rio, the Odeon. It's Q's attention to inanimate objects which draws women in their droves. He has practised all his subtle, clandestine stroking of everyday household fixtures, choreographed the spiralling index finger, dragging nail, the sweep of his palm, he has perfected the gestures of desire.

But it's not only suggestive gestures which have encouraged such drooling adulation. Q's voice, sweet and dark, can be tasted. It can whisper words of passion, confess to terrible secrets or utter something as banal as *I'm looking for employment* and a breathless, female sigh will ripple through an auditorium. To be honest, Q could recite a page of the telephone directory and create the same effect.

The schnapps is going to my head. We ordered our blinis ages ago but no sign of them so far. Drinking on an empty stomach's never a good idea. The dead woman drank herself to death. Or drowned. Or both. But whatever the body expired from, the spirit had already had the life squeezed out of it. Does Fraser have the same capacity for cruelty as the dead woman's husband? Or Nick, or Philip? This isn't a rational thought, I know, just a nasty black flicker in my head.

As I'm the only one of us who's come close to meeting Q before, Fraser has been nagging me to ask him over.

Like many men, of either persuasion, he claims not to understand what women see in Q. However, Fraser's addiction to success tends to outweigh personal taste; he consumes it like other people eat pizza, and can sound knowledgeable about productions he's never seen. Sitting next to me, stroking his trim little beard and looking as fresh as he did when we left the flat this morning, I realise that, though we've been together for five years, there are huge areas of Fraser's life that I know very little about. His work and the people he knows through it are usually dispensed with in the time it takes to remove his jacket and switch on the TV. Computing isn't the easiest subject for small talk but I have tried. Fraser just doesn't give much away.

Q doesn't look as if he wants company, or, for that matter, if he'd be much fun. Gloomy and preoccupied, he's faithful to the dark, brooding persona his fans can't get enough of. He's never been one for comedy.

Fraser: I think Q looks lonely.
Nick: If I were him, I'd be bored by now. I can never bear more than half a drink in my own company.
Philip: Drinking alone begins as a bid for independence but turns into an exercise in loneliness.
Nick: You don't go to a bar to be alone, do you?
Fraser: Maybe he's waiting for someone.
Nick: Looks like the someone's kept him waiting long enough.
Me: All right!

Q is staring into the middle distance and scrupulously avoiding eye contact with anyone. My choice is to shout or touch. As I detest raising my voice unless I'm being paid for it, I reach over and tap the shoulder of his soft, mole-brown coat. Close up, in the flesh, Q has plenty of plain, ordinary angles as well as the familiar photogenic ones. Being short, I have an intimate view of his nostrils which are no more appealing than anyone else's.

He seems pleased enough that I came over to speak to him though he doesn't remember me from the time we almost met and I misquote the title of his latest film. Our conversation begins with the usual – Are you working, what are you working on now, what are you working on next? against a wall of background noise; glasses being thrust into scalding water, the bleeping till, a fruit machine vomiting coins. Q's voice arcs through the racket, a soft curve of sound swings towards me until I notice a platter of blinis on its way to the table and Fraser beckoning impatiently.

Once the introductions are done – Q is obliged to do a lot of manly hand-shaking – we dig into the food. The blinis are fresh and hot and reassuringly stodgy. I'm half-way through my second before I realise how hungry I am. And still, in spite of more schnapps, chittering.

Fraser: She's had a hard day.

Fraser claps me heartily on the back, like a dog. Q nods. His lips crinkle in my direction.

Nick: Haven't we all. God, I want to go back to making commercials; something wholesome, like breakfast cereal or vitamin supplements, or gardening tools. No, not gardening tools. What am I saying? The last time I did gardening tools, the clapperloader fell off a ladder and impaled herself on a hedge clipper.

Already Nick is talking too loud.

Nick: You like this place?
Q: It's handy.
Nick: Right! So you live nearby?
Q: Not far away.
Nick: Whereabouts? This is home territory, man.
Q: I try not to publicise my address.
Nick: Quite right, too. Keep the fans at bay. Protect your privacy.
Q: It's not that . . .
Nick: He's just being modest, isn't he? I bet he can't walk down the street without some obsessed female stalking him. By the way, this woman we've been working on had most of your films on video.
Q: I have to go.
Nick: You've only just sat down! You're not superstitious are you? Let me buy you a drink. I haven't even bought you a drink.
Q: My wife . . .
Nick: Say no more. Half an hour late and the wife goes spare. Do I remember that shit. Used to drive me bonkers, having to account for every minute as if I were under contract. Glad to say, I'm no longer accountable.

Nick's cheeks are flushed – from the schnapps or the fire – and his eyes are worryingly bright. It's not quite a year since his wife left him for a quiet but punctual librarian.

Q: My wife . . . needs me. And I need her.

Since we left the pub, I haven't stopped shivering. On the tube we perched stiffly on our seats, intent on the Somali family across the aisle; stoic, impassive parents and sleepy children who pressed their pretty heads against the dirty upholstery. Fraser is annoyed; with Q, maybe, for rushing off so quickly or with Nick for prompting Q's departure, or me for having a star to myself for five minutes, I don't know but I don't like the way he's crashing about in the kitchen looking for something else to eat and cracking open another beer. If he'd just come right out with what's bugging him instead of transmitting his bad mood through the floorboards . . .

My head hurts; nothing drastic, just a dull kind of hung-over throbbing. The steam from the bath I'm running has fogged up the mirror so I can't see whether or not my new hairstyle is an improvement. My neck feels naked, exposed. Though I'm alone and the bathroom door is locked, I can't shake off the sensation that there's someone behind me . . .

The dead woman must have felt like that almost all the time. She must have looked over her shoulder for years, quaking at the sound of her husband's footsteps. A small, weaselish man, fast and vicious. His explosive rages left her shaking for days at a time. The bathroom, with its puny snib, was her refuge, hot water and vodka her comforters. The husband had to break the lock to discover her body but – according to the sister – breaking things was something he was good at. The bathwater was cold, the vodka bottle empty. The husband summoned the police immediately, leaving the submerged corpse of his wife fingerprint-free for the law to deal with. Her damp, farewell note – *I'm so sorry, Marguerite* – was on the shelf, under the tooth mug.

I wipe the mirror with my hand and see a tired, shorn woman fading as more steam adheres to the surface of the cold glass. I turn off the taps and slide down into the hot, comforting water and do what countless women do; close my eyes and think of Q, backlit, mouthing seductive, rehearsed words.

Beyond Vigilance

HIS HAND WAS hot, dry and covered in curly black hairs. He wore a chunky silver ring on his middle finger. His teeth were white and even, eyes shadowy behind tinted glasses. His black jacket was shot through with silver threads. He smelled of garlic and a recently applied sour-sweet cologne. Susie snuffled up to him like a puppy, pawing at his free hand, gazing at him in adoration, yapping non-stop.

—Sam, Sam, I know a joke. Let me tell you a joke . . .

You could still feel the heat in your palm when you removed your hand. He had one of those handshakes, that reassuring squeeze you'd never quite trusted. Too keen somehow to evince trustworthiness. You wanted rid of him before Billy got back to the bar.

The bar was busy. A crowd of flax-haired Icelandic tourists were listening, with boozy tolerance, to an interminable speech by a fat man in a hat. The PA was playing up; the mike swallowed the speaker's voice, chewed it and spat it out as garble and feedback. There were kids everywhere.

You'd met Sam that morning, in the lift, on your way to the pool. Susie had been wearing her swimsuit – dayglo pink – which gave her pale skin a greenish tinge. Under the lift's harsh light she looked luminous, spritish. Sam and another man were already in the lift when the two of you squeezed in. They were speaking Spanish, a language barely heard in the hotel. It was better to listen to, easier on the ear than the usual rattling French, measured German and whining English. As the lift descended, the men's conversation switched to Susie, who giggled and squirmed under their appraising eyes. They liked what they saw; Susie knew it and loved it. When the word 'sexy' jumped out from their stream of Spanish, you pulled her close, tried to hide her behind you. But Susie didn't want to be hidden from admirers; at least not youngish, dapper, smiling ones.

—Your little girl is very . . . pretty, said Sam. When she grow up, she will break the hearts.

—Sam, Sam!

—Yes, my honey?

—Why do bees have sticky hair?

—You have sticky hair? You have some ice cream in it?

—No, it's a joke. You've got to say: *I don't know. Why do bees have sticky hair?*

—Why do bees have sticky hair?

—Because they comb it with a honeycomb!

Susie screeched at her own joke. Sam flashed his teeth and patted her head. He didn't get it.

—Don't bother the man, Susie, you said. He's got work to do.

—It is no bother, Madame. I *love* children. And your little girl, I think she *love* me, yes?

—Susie, why don't you go and play with that wee girl you saw at the pool this morning.

—I don't want to play. I want to be with Sam.

—OK, my honey, said Sam. You want to see me make disco?

Susie clapped her hands, blinked like a stunned rabbit

and skipped after him before you could think of a reason why she shouldn't.

—Stay where I can see you.

Spain loves kids, Billy had said, which is why you'd decided on a week in Majorca. The resort was certainly geared up to kids as consumers. On the main drag – an endless narrow street permanently choked with anarchic traffic – every other shop sold ice cream and trashy plastic toys twirled beneath striped awnings. Apart from the poolside and a shabby, weed-strewn beach at the other end of town, there was nowhere much for kids to play.

Today, though, you'd finally found a little swing park at the end of a backstreet of low white houses and broad-leaved trees. Late afternoon and the bleached colours of the day were deepening, local life was beginning to resume slowly after siesta. There were no other parents in the park, just a few Spanish kids noisily clambering over each other on the climbing frame and chucking rocks down the chute. Susie ran towards them, fell and grazed her knee. After a thorough inspection of her injury – which was slight – she took a turn on everything but in a wary, joyless way. There were no safety surfaces here, just rubble laced with broken glass and her usual confidence had taken a knock. The Spanish kids had no interest in her which made her embarrassed and self-conscious and keen to get back to the pool.

It was when you were leaving the park that you came across the wee lost boy, hunkered down in the dirt, bawling. His face was blotched with tears, mud and rage. A damp nappy sagged below his shorts. Susie knelt down beside him, asked him where his mummy was and tried to give him a cuddle but the boy pushed her away and kept on roaring.

Susie had wanted to take him to the police station but neither you nor Billy knew where it was and, anyway, trying to shift the child didn't seem like a good idea. He was upset enough as it was without some foreign strangers trying to lift him up. These days, at home, people thought twice about approaching any child, even a lost one. Billy did go back over to the swings and tried, with the few Spanish words he knew, to ask the other kids whether the child was with them. They gawped at him in bewilderment, leaped down from the climbing frame and ran off.

Who knows how long you'd have dithered, had an old woman not made it her business to leave the doorstep she had been mopping and scuff across the street in her slippers. All three of you began babbling at once, trying to explain, to ask for help. Her eyes quizzed each of you in turn, then, laughing at your hopeless Spanish, your worried faces, she swept the lost boy up from the dirt and clamped him on to a broad hip.

—*Llamo a Mama. OK, OK.*

You watched as she padded sturdily across the road – causing the traffic to jolt to a halt – talking non-stop to the boy and fending off his hysterical fists with smiles. When she reached her doorstep, she turned and waved.

—*Adiós.*

You walked to the hotel, glancing back from time to time.

—All the kids in that swing park were too young to be out without a grown-up, said Susie, echoing the fearful arrangements of home.

—It's a bit different here, said Billy.

—How?

—Because Spain likes kids.

—Why was nobody watching that tiny wee boy, then?

You and Billy sat on stools, facing the stage.

—Where's Susie? said Billy.

—She's fine.

—But where is she?

—With the DJ.

You pointed to the back of the stage where Sam was trailing an extension cable behind a heavy curtain. Without hesitation, Susie followed him.

—She's OK.

—How can you tell? said Billy. You can't even see her!

Susie darted in and out of the stage curtain. Sam patted her head indulgently as he went about his preparations but he was clearly more interested in shaking the hands and kissing the cheeks of the tall Icelandic women who, now that their speechmaker had finished, were free to circulate.

—I don't want her hanging around that smoothie, said Billy.

—Susie's pestering him, not the other way round.

—Just look at him. Bloody gigolo if you ask me.

—He's OK. He came up and said hello.

—Did he now. How very nice of him.

The disco music was too loud and awful. A handful of teenage girls sloped on to the floor and jerked about half-heartedly. A wee boy in shirt and bow tie waltzed with his granny. While Sam was busy spinning discs which appealed to no one, Susie and some other kids ran out to the poolside to hunt for snails.

It was not one of those sunken kidney bowls but an old-fashioned rectangular pool with a high stone wall. Flowering shrubs sprouted through the pointing, home to colonies of ants, beetles and snails. The wee kids, like Susie, contented themselves with poking around the wall. The bigger ones clambered on to it, daring each other to teeter along it a few screeching steps.

You were usually the one who couldn't relax but tonight it was Billy who was on and off his bar stool, checking on Susie, telling her off for fooling around – though all the kids were running wild – and grumbling about the time when nobody else seemed the least bit ready for bed. Earlier in the holiday, you'd made a point of not keeping her up till all hours because the sun tired her out, the sun and the little differences in everything. And when she reached a certain point she didn't give in; she fought against tiredness, sense and the will of grown-ups.

But you'd promised, promised her a bit of freedom. It wasn't something kids had much any more, at home. And if they did, it was called neglect. You couldn't take the risk any more. If you read the papers, watched the news, you couldn't trust anybody – neighbours, friends, family even. That wee lost boy in the park. Had you done the right thing to hand him over to a stranger, even a local stranger who seemed kind and capable?

Sam had taken a break from the disco, which made it possible to talk without yelling in Billy's ear. It also meant that Susie deserted her pals and trailed after her idol. She was worn out. Her eyelids drooped, she was tripping over her own feet and talking drivel.

—Let's go, said Billy. She's had her bit of disco

– didn't even dance. I'm not sitting through another session of that crap.

—It's not fair! Susie wailed. You promised I could stay up. And Sam promised he'd walk me round the pool!

—We can do it another time, my honey, said Sam.

—No, no! I'm going home tomorrow and I'll never see you again, ever.

You wait by the shallow end, in shadow. At the deep end, Billy stands guard. It's quiet outside now and the bay, spanned by paths of rosy light from distant hotels, bars and discos, looks prettier than it does by day. The pool is glassy. On the far side, beyond its black sheen, you can see Susie and the man in silhouette, hand in hand, edging along the high narrow wall.

Rope

THE LEATHER LEASHES are taut as rigged hawsers. The man strains to match the force of their muzzled heads and harnessed shoulders. They're taking him for a walk, these muscle-bound, rock-skulled dogs with boiled red eyes and drooling jaws. These are no pets in the ordinary sense; not cuddly beasts with which an animal lover might share a bit of harmless rough and tumble, not fluffy mutts which lope after sticks and balls and deposit them at the feet of an approving master, begging for claps on warm compliant heads and the game to begin again.

Nothing at all is compliant about this pair, nothing tamed except by force. It's in his every step, the strain of control, of keeping these power-packs in check; these bald brutes pitting their wills against his. His belted mac perfectly matches their own coats, close-cropped, colourless as putty.

To love animals like these takes something other than delight. There is nothing to love in these dogs unless you can count devotion to their transparent savagery, their naked ugliness; every step the man takes is one of restraint, of struggle for control. If the bitch's lead goes slack, if she pauses to sniff the soiled municipal turf or if the dog thrusts thuggishly at a whimsical, parkwise squirrel, it is all the man can do to keep them in check.

Like the dogs, the boy, too, moves from the shoulders, as if he sees some aggro ahead, something to square up to, as if he's going to hit something head-on, though there's only his dad's tightly belted back, his dad clenched in the steel grip of his will, his dad's body hard, unyielding, buttoned up against the elements.

The boy doesn't mind the cold. The winter wind scrabbles through his outsize lumberjack shirt. He shivers at the thrill of it nipping his chest, scratching at his belly, his belt buckle. On either side of his dad he sees Cass and Tara's thin, bare tails twitch as they walk, stick up from squat, wagging bums, porking the foggy air like it's flesh.

Flesh: that word. He just has to say the word and he imagines Chantelle trotting ahead of him, Chantelle with her pale lips and arched black eyebrows, her pointy tits and long, long legs. He feels hungry. A burger would hit the spot; meat, melted cheese and a soft, spongy roll; something to put in his mouth. If he had something to put in his mouth he wouldn't have to think about Chantelle's body or dogs' tails porking the fog.

The boy needs a haircut; his thick fringe swings into his puppy eyes as he shoulders forward, shirt-tail flapping, trainer laces trailing. It will be his turn soon, his shot. His dad will wrap the leashes round his gloved palms until the dogs are half-choked, until their tongues go purple and slop out of their mouths. Then his dad will hand the dogs over to him.

He has to go through this stuff with the dogs; it's crap and sometimes he moans about it but there's no point, there's no way around it. It's Friday and he wants money. His dad will hand over a fiver.

—If you've shown some progress with the dogs, son. I want to see some progress.

There was always this progress thing, this way his dad had of measuring him up, even though you never got to see it in his face. You couldn't tell anything from his dad's face about how he felt; it hardly moved. Even when he spoke, his face looked frozen and grey, like his coat.

You've got to have money in your pocket. Chantelle always has loads of money. In the lunchbreak, she flashes her cash about and treats her pals to cream cakes. One time he was standing right behind her in the baker's, in the queue for filled rolls and pizza. With all the jostling going on, it was easy to rub up against her short tight skirt, accidentally on purpose. He just about came on the spot.

Chantelle hardly knows he exists. And if she knew, if she knew what he did while he chants her name over and over? Jeer, probably, or pity him and one is as bad as the other. Chantelle doesn't go with schoolboys; she's into men. Men are into Chantelle. Boys are dross to Chantelle but one day he'd show her, one day he'd give her one, ram her right up the crack. She'd be down on the grass, laughing and trying to fight him off with scorn. He'd pin her down so she'd have to kick and bite and scratch but he'd be strong, and rock-hard. Her skirt would ride up her thighs as he pulled down her pants in one easy movement and then he'd be up there, up inside her . . .

His dad is pushing his biscuit-coloured hair out of his eyes. The boy has forgotten the colour of his dad's eyes. They're just dark gaps, gashes in his face. His dad's eyes are not looking out or in, they're looking away, always looking away, even now when he calls him over, yanks him out of the Chantelle fantasy and back to the sweaty smell of the dogs, to their thonged leashes cutting into his dad's thick gloves, their short strangled pants as they gasp for more rope, his dad's faraway groan, his dad's hands clasping his own, the leather rope between them. There was always this thing between them, this thing handed from father to son.

As soon as his dad lets go, the dogs tear off. They're making for a tree – head-butting's a favourite trick – but instead of charging it together, they split up at the last moment, forking at the tree and dragging him hard against the trunk, stretching his legs and arms like the bands of a catapult, scraping his nose, chin, belly against the rough bark. His bare hands burn. Why doesn't he get to wear gloves, like his dad? His eyes burn too, prickle with tears but he won't cry out, won't howl in pain, bawl at the dogs or his dad, won't let the shame show.

Folk are looking. Folk are laughing. His dad is laughing. The dogs are bastards, doing this to him when there are people about. People have stopped to look and point him out to each other. His dad's a bastard, standing there watching and laughing.

—Need a hand, son?

—Nuh.

—You've scuppered yourself, son.

—I'm OK, right!

—You need a bit more control, another wee lesson in leash management.

He isn't giving in. He's had it with giving in, had it with his dad's wee lessons. He'll just hang on like this, jammed up against the tree like a fucking clown until the dogs stop straining, until there's a bit of slack from one of them.

* * *

His dad's lessons took place out the back, in the concrete yard where dandelions and thistles burst through the cracks. It felt like prison, being marched around with the dogs, his dad ordering him about, barred in by windows on all sides. The dogs had their kennel in the yard and the run, well it was a big cage really, with a dirty great padlock on the steel door. His dad built it. He held pliers and hammers and bags of screws. When Tara had her pups – just the one litter – his dad threw in a couple of blankets. The pups were sold and then the vet sorted her. The vet said he could fix Cass too so he wouldn't strain so hard at the leash but his dad didn't want that. His dad thought that was cruel, though he whipped the dog often enough for it.

—Grip it like this son, close to the body, son, grip it like your life depended on it. Let them know who's boss.

He knows fine who's boss right now, who's always bloody boss. His dad just won't accept it, won't see that it's all he can do to stay on his feet, never mind trying to make the bastards walk to heel. But this is what they do; night after night they pretend that one day he'll take over, take his dad's place, put on the gloves and tighten the muzzles, clip on the leads and hit the streets, a team to be reckoned with.

It had to happen when there are all these folk out for the shows, drifting through the fog with their bouncy balloons and puke-pink teddy bears. He can see the lights, their colours milky in the fog, and hear a muffled mess of noise; squealing voices, roaring machinery, thudding music. Some of his pals have been to the shows already. Others will be there tonight. Pug told him about a new ride, the Terminator, which swings up really fast and high and all the girls' skirts fly up. If you stand in the right place, you can see everything. Chantelle might be there. He'd like to watch Chantelle on the Terminator, or anything else. He'd like to watch her being tossed about, squealing.

The rides make him sick and the sideshows are crap but he likes the food smells; burgers, onions, candy floss, popcorn, all the warm, sweet, greasy smells. He likes the crowds, likes being in the thick of people, the closeness. And the noise. Once you're in there, the noise is like a wall, blotting everything else out. But the noise is still too far away to blot out the dogs, yapping and panting on either side of the tree and not fucking budging an inch.

—I've better things to do than stay here all night, son.

—Me too.

—Call it a day, son. Just call it a day.

His dad is flexing his fingers in a showy, self-important way. His dad likes people to see his thick black gloves which make his hands look too big for his body, make them slow and clumsy and evil-looking, like the mechanical mitts of a robot.

The only chance to get free of this tug-of-war with the dogs is to go for one at a time. Cass is on his right. The dog is stronger than the bitch but his right arm's stronger than his left, so he wedges his left arm against the tree and tugs on the right with everything he's got and he can see it happening, he can see the bastard turn tail and trot towards him but it's too late to stop the pulling. He wheels round the tree, lands flat on his back in the wet grass and there's a shadow above him closing in, and the shadow raises its feet and stamps on his open hands. And then his dad's gloved hands reach down and clamp around the leashes before he lifts his feet.

The boy tries to shake the slimy leaves off his clothes but they cling on, like shreds of wet skin and he has to peel them off one by one; they leave behind gouts of greasy mud. The shirt is ruined. It's his favourite; a real American skateboarding shirt from the best place in town. Weeks, no months, he'd saved up for it, served his time out the back with his dad and the dogs and now it's gubbed. He presses his fingers into his armpits. He's finished with it all, finished. He'll never get to grips with the handling. And doesn't want to. His thumb's rigid. Maybe it's broken. Maybe his dad's broken his thumb. Maybe he should go to hospital. He's surrounded by hospitals. To the left, near the school, is the Royal. To the right, bang up against his old primary, is the Sick Kids. He's been there a few times when he was wee, quite a few. He got to know the nurses and some of them were OK, kind, but he's too old for the Sick Kids now.

His dad and the dogs are plodding on. Their breaths echo, make holes in the fog. His dad holds his head high and stiff. The dogs, cowed by the whipping they got from his dad, walk to heel, their hurt noses skimming the ground. The team dissolves slowly, melts away. The boy stays where he is. They're not his dogs. It's not his life.

But [illegible] to make [illegible] with the [illegible] and [illegible] to know the names [illegible] of them were OK and [illegible] [illegible] [illegible]

[illegible] and the [illegible]

Limo

THE WHITE STRETCH limo is sinking into the mud. If Logan doesn't get some planks under the tyres, it'll sink so deep he'll need to hire a forklift to get it back on the road, the rutted track which even a jeep finds hard-going. Blue leather seats, pale blue. Powder blue, Logan says, popular in the Presley era. Before my time. If you tug a flap, the back seat pulls out into a king-size divan. Powder-blue blinds slip out of the padded roof and clip on to little metal studs. Sometimes they slip off the studs and spring back up again and Logan curses, colourful full-bodied curses most folk haven't the energy for. With his deep, dark voice he delivers them but Logan's curses do not have anything to do with his anger.

When Logan is angry, his voice shuts down completely. Words snag and rasp in his throat, dry and scratchy and I listen to the dew drip from the rhododendrons which are rambling over the car, burying it in dark green dribbles.

My head is pressed against the cool blue blind. Logan is running his thumb down my back, pressing the vertebrae one by one, all the way down. His thumb circles the lowest bone and I wriggle and imagine a tail, a tail which could twitch and curl and slap his heavy hand away. I would like a tail, a real one. Not that horsehair thing Logan brought back from Soho. Not that – it's fake and stupid and I stuck it on my head like a wig instead of where he wanted me to put it.

If he really wants a pony, there are plenty in the stables. Pretty speckled ponies, shipped from Argentina or Arizona, I've forgotten but somewhere hot and dry. They trek around in mud here, most of the time, slogging up slippery tracks, their hooves rotting, while bulky beginners whip their haunches, kick their sides and yank on the reins. I never ride. Sometimes I go to the stables to smell the sweet piss-wet hay, to feel the ponies' steamy breath on my face, to look into their big troubled eyes. On cold days they cough and shiver under their blankets and I am sad for them.

There's rain, today – usually there's rain, which makes it green here, and beautiful – and Donny the piper is wheezing into action as dawn crawls over the hills. Not the piper's fault, morning, I know, he's only doing his job and if Milly could think of some better way to start her day, the students could get some peace in the mornings, not to mention those of us who also live here all year round without a suite of rooms in the west wing and an uninterrupted view of the islands. Logan says being woken by a piper is Milly's only extravagance. He says Milly hates the sound of the pipes so much that she gets out of bed to shut Donny up. People are strange.

Dawn, in the rain; the piper on the grass in full highland dress underneath his dripping cagoule, playing another of his rousing laments. I wrap my blanket around my shoulders and sneak down the horse-track to the shore, leaving Logan to tidy up his limo. Sneak. Not my word for it but one overheard: *I saw her sneaking down the track this morning, Logan, at dawn, in a blanket, barefoot. What the hell was she up to, creeping about the place?* Milly. He says she doesn't know about him and me and if she did, she wouldn't care too much. Milly cares about paying the bills. Milly is too beat at night to want him near her, he says. She might even be glad, he says. I can't imagine Milly glad. Too much stone in her, too much endurance; no gladness left. Milly has no desire and, Logan says, no appetite for games.

Logan, I think, lives for games. Sometimes one of his games is such fun that I laugh too loud and he has to put his hands over my mouth. And then that becomes another game. There are good games and bad games and some very boring games as well. The limo is where we play them, me and Logan, the limo which can't go anywhere until Logan gets his road built. When he gets his road built, he wants to use the car as a swish taxi service for the students. He says I should learn to drive. Milly would buy me a tartan suit and a frilly blouse with pearl buttons and I could pick up the students from the railway station. I used to know how to drive but I've forgotten. And I don't want to meet anybody off the train.

You'll never know. You can see the contours of the islands; their fleshy curves, the soft pinks and greys, milky blues – the colour of a breast, an eyelid – the gradual slip from light to dark, you can see but you'll never know. You trek down with your sketchbooks, cameras, greedy eyes noting line, tone, the misty fingers of land. You search for the perfect angle, considering whether the gull which wheels between you and the view might be captured in a couple of swift, reckless brushstrokes or whether such a sudden, living movement might mar the composition. Your sturdy all-weather walking shoes crunch over the shingle, crushing lilac crabs and sea pinks underfoot. Piss off.

*　*　*

Some days here it's just never-ending grey. I like those days. Nobody comes clattering over my bit of beach when it's grey and damp. The seaweed smells good. The tide has washed the shore clean. I don't want any of your shitty litter on my beach, not a scrap, OK? Not a ring-pull, a fag end, nothing. Only the litter of history for me; bleached bone, smashed china, shattered glass, trundled by the tide into cool smooth jewels.

The students come and go. Just faces round the table, voices. A name or two makes itself known to me though I make no effort to know it. No need. All day working on the assignments they've been given and in the evening, they can't wait to get at the food, at Milly's pretty dishes, Milly's own little works of art. I cart the veg from the kitchen to the dining room where Logan is carving the meat, smooth, thick slices of breast and leg, for those who eat it. Between us, we pile on the nosh and get back to the kitchen.

Milly sloshes pots in the sink. Logan hums tunelessly, scrapes plates and slams them down on the draining board. Milly has a way of scowling which makes you feel like her life is your fault. Mostly, she's cross at Logan but everybody else has to put up with her crappy moods too. Maybe, if Milly hadn't been so sour from the start, I'd never have seen inside Logan's powder-blue limo. She never liked me. Maybe she knows Logan too well, knows the tracks his mind takes him down, dark thorny paths which all lead to the limo. His mind stays locked behind the blue blinds while he serves up Milly's food and listens to everybody rave about it. Milly is a very good cook. Tonight a woman clawed my arm with her blood-red nails to tell me how good Milly's cooking is. I hate that, a person taking hold of me like that. I don't know why. I've forgotten why.

Logan needs to fix up the dining-room ceiling. The cornice and centre rose are hanging from threads of plaster, like garlands left over from a dance. They used to have dances here but now it's courses, courses, courses. A few more courses, all those feet dunting the floor – one day the rose will come crashing down on Milly's wonderful food. I never eat Milly's food. Usually I serve it and help with the dishes but Thursday is the life class and once the coffee's done I'm in the toilet, undressing for the benefit of this week's students.

Kyle, the course tutor, says he's asked Logan more than once to fix up a proper changing room. I believe him. I always believe Kyle. I don't know why really, maybe because he has no reason to lie to me, or because his voice is high and light, girlish almost, or because he reminds me of somebody, it doesn't matter. But so far, it's still the crappy kitchen toilet with the broken window and midges whirling in when I switch on the light.

The studio is filling up. Easels scrape across the floor. The heater hums. Already, there's a hot flush of anticipation as the students set up, jostling for a good view of the empty dais, its scatter of cushions. They've been reproducing sunsets and tree lines all week, mottled urns, pearly shells, sedge grass, dead crabs, bladderwrack, the roofless watermill, half-buried still, the rusted catch of a redundant gate, a mossed panel of drystane dyke, all in painstaking detail, but tonight their subject is a living body, a nude: me.

Kyle has offered me one of the kimonos he uses for

background colour to wear between the toilet and the studio, a black one with tangerines on it or a blue one with lime-green hummingbirds but I prefer my scabby old blanket. It smells of smoke and salt, of home.

When Logan found out that I lived in a cave, he offered me a caravan, like Kyle's, but nearer the big house. Milly didn't say anything except that I could use their facilities; a washing machine would clean my clothes better than the sea and surely a hot shower would be nice? Milly worries about the guests complaining about me and wrinkles her nose when I come into work, checking to see that I smell OK. She hates my clothes. Almost every week she reminds me that MacRae's do a cheap, smart line in polyester, machine-washable skirts. More than once she's offered to drive me to town – on pay day – but I never go. I think about a trip in the jeep but Milly curses worse than Logan when she's behind the wheel and it's been so long now . . .

It's not the town I don't like, it's no worse than any other, no better either, except that it's by the sea and the ferries come and go from the mainland to the islands and the gulls make as much noise as the people; big, fat, well-fed gulls which loop around the docks. But no city, town, village, no place big enough to have a name is for me. Not now.

But Milly's right about the shower. Sometimes when it's damp like this I feel so chilled, as if my body is packed in ice, like a killed fish, and I shudder and shake and can't hold the pose. Kyle is kind. He turns up the heater until the room is hot and the students start to sweat – well, they say it's the heat as they loosen collars, roll up sleeves and drag limp hankies across pink foreheads. But some sweat at the sight of a naked body – no, a *nude* body – stretched out on the couch. Kyle says there's a difference between nakedness and nudity. I don't think there is but he's the teacher and he pays for nudity. Logan must think there's a difference too because he doesn't pay for nakedness.

At the life class nobody talks. The room holds its breath; all its energy is concentrated in a dozen sharpened sticks. Sometimes I can tell by the sound of charcoal dragging across paper which part of me they're drawing; long flowing strokes for legs and arms, finicky flicks and dabs for head, hands and feet, an intense, concentrated rubbing and scratching for the crotch.

Kyle picks his way through the easels, stopping to comment on a line, an angle, a patch of shading. *Draw what you see,* he says, *not what you know.* He says this time and again in his kind, papery voice, without sounding bored of repeating himself. I'm standing, holding a broomstick above my head, left leg bent, right leg stretched back. Liberation, Kyle calls the pose – it hurts like hell. I count seconds and minutes and concentrate on keeping still. After a bit, Logan slips into the studio, pretending to hunt for stray coffee mugs left over from the afternoon's bowl-and-bottle exercise. It's his excuse to sneak a look at the sketches. Sometimes I think these crude likenesses of me whet his appetite more than the real thing.

Milly never ever comes into the studio but I can picture her scowling in the kitchen and can't help laughing. The broomstick wobbles. Chairs scrape, the students keek round their easels to stare at me laughing at nothing. I'm supposed to be looking up at the bloody broom I'm trying to hold steady, looking liberatedly upwards but I hear them turn to each other and nod. Laughing out loud at nothing is what madwomen do and I must, after all, be mad.

Lives in a cave, you know, along the beach. No facilities whatsoever. A city kid, on the run. It's just not natural, is it? Somewhere warm you could almost imagine it for a while but here, for so long, in this sodden climate? Must be touched. Wanders around at night, too, half-dressed, bedraggled. I'd lock my door if I were you.

It's true, I don't sleep much at night. Other things to do, always other things to do. There must have been a time when I slept like other people, but I can't remember; it's gone, lost. Long after the students have gone off to their rooms and locked their doors in case the madwoman goes walkabout, I pose in the limo, for Logan. Unlike my liberated, nude poses for Kyle, the naked compositions which Logan suggests are modelled more on the style of *Knave* or *Fiesta* than *Amateur Artist.* Logan has no intention of trying to capture a likeness on paper and I don't have to hold his poses for nearly as long as some of Kyle's but . . . Logan has become so greedy for sensation.

She pokes a finger under a smooth stone, overturns it and crouches down until her face is inches from the damp dark sand. The shore life which she has disturbed moves haphazardly, confused by sudden exposure to light, air. Raking through the wetness, she picks up a crab the size of her fingernail, blows on it to dislodge some of the sand, pops it into her mouth, feels it scuttle frantically over her tongue, spits it out again and laughs into the still, early morning air. Her voice slithers across the shingle. She follows her own laughter to the water's edge where the sea folds in like a cool smooth sheet. She stretches out on the shingle, face down. There is no one to witness her nakedness, her first-light prostration. Barnacles graze her breasts, nick her ribs. At her navel, something slimy clings and oozes. Her pelvis is jammed against a sharp rock. Gripping two large boulders, she drags herself forward, feeling the tug and scrape along the skinny length of herself, until her face is at the tideline: stones, water, sky, a pall of midges. She opens her mouth wide as a cave and the grey sea floods in. She holds the sea in her mouth for as long as her lungs will permit.

Verge

HE COULD ALMOST touch the hedgerows on either side of the road. His eyes prickled. There was too much to see, the space insufficient, scale minute. All that sizzling, crawling and spawning: it was too close, too vivid and exhausting, like the flutters, twitches and scrabbles of a bad hangover. He wanted to push the hedgerows back to a safe, impressionistic blur.

The car was long out of sight, back down the vermicular road, clapped-out on a narrow heel of gravel which called itself a passing place. The next vehicle to scoot round the bend would probably prang it. If there was one. He'd seen nothing on the road since he'd left the village but parallel curves of hedgerow and, overhead, a narrow ribbon of sky. There was a lack of air, as if the teeming hawthorn and briar had sucked it all up, leaving only a sour-sweet odour, a sickly mix of the blossoming and decomposing. The turgid heat pressed at his temples. He was burning up with thirst. There was always the sherry. Not wanting to return empty-handed – and subject himself to Margot's scorn – he'd brought along a bottle of Fino. The rest of the booze he'd bought in the village was locked in the car boot. A slug of sherry was better than nothing; it might at least take the edge off what promised to be a long walk. He hardly ever walked these days, other than a brief digestive stroll after one of Margot's healthy meals or a meandering toddle with wee Gayle.

They'd come to be near the sea but, here, he might as well be worlds away from the cheering breeze and the languid contours of coastline from which, on a clear day, you could see Land's End. The cliffs must be somewhere nearby, but where? He hadn't bargained for roads like this at all, expected a bit more from this part of the world.

What was the point of going somewhere different if you couldn't see the scenery?

Margot's heart had been set on somewhere foreign, a French chateau, Italian *palazzo* – Margot's imagination inclined to the grand cliché – but he'd put his foot down; nothing difficult. No use making a holiday harder work than everyday life. Not going along with Margot's daydream had meant being lumbered with brochures to study at breakfast and dinner conversation – the only time he and Margot had what might pass for conversation – was confined to locations and facilities. Still, talking about holiday homes was better than talking about Iris.

The children were needing to eat. No matter how often Margot asked them nicely not to shout all at once and told them that crying couldn't cure anything, it made no difference. Running about all day in such relentless heat, it was no wonder they were fractious but they wouldn't be told, wouldn't just stay indoors and settle to some restful activity. She would have happily accommodated them at the kitchen table if only they'd let her get on with the food. Her sister's children seemed totally committed to tormenting each other and Gayle was fretting for Finlay's return.

Since they'd arrived, Gayle hadn't let Grandad out of her sight without a protracted, dramatic farewell. Today she'd pleaded and whined for Finlay to take her along to the village, five slow miles away. The child was entranced by the place. Straight out of a picture book – thatched cottages with blowsy pink roses all but concealing doorways – it hung over a tidal inlet where fat ducks bobbed on the swell and the water sparkled like a fairytale.

Grandad had got to go on his own for once but God knows what promises the child had extracted from him: a trip to see the pig, the pony, yet another swim in the slimy, disappointing pool. For a man accustomed to calling the shots, Finlay was indulgent to the point of idiocy with Gayle when she so clearly required a firm hand. Never never never would Margot wish any harshness to be inflicted on her darling granddaughter but there had to be limits, guidelines, something to fall back on. If she and Finlay didn't provide them, the child was bound to grow up reckless and adrift. It would only be a matter of time before she was drawn into a swamp of deviant sex, drugs and the inevitable despair of any motherless child.

Guidelines, security, these were things that she and Finlay could take care of with their eyes shut. They couldn't, even under present circumstances, create an impression of a loving couple – that was a long way back down the road. Yet, though their mutual contempt was public and energetic, there was still a private place in each of them where another kind of love struggled to survive.

It was hard to believe; only a few hours down the M8 then off west but even his basic idea of landscape had gone by the board. There was just nothing to see except the dense, bristling hedgerows which rose high above his head. Beyond them there must be fields of peas and wheat, rolling, springy downs, wiry sheep. It was getting dark. He would be late back, no question. Instead of swigging warm sherry from a bottle, he should be on the patio by now, a Scotch on ice cool in his hand, working up an appetite as the stunning heat of the day gave way to a mellow evening glow. They had been bloody lucky with the weather; not a wisp of cloud since they arrived, which was just as well with the screaming kids to contend with. A tonic in their way, the wee ones – and welcome company for Gayle – but there's only so much you can take of what's good for you, a lesson he'd learned from a lifetime with Margot.

He would miss his few minutes' peace, lounging under the rampant clematis while Margot worked wonders in the kitchen, wonders of which, at fifty-nine, he was still ignorant. How long would it be before somebody noticed that he had been gone too long? And who would it be: Gayle, Margot, or one of the in-laws Margot had invited to share their holiday because the two of them were precious little company for each other?

Through the open French windows, she could hear ice crack in glasses and wasps fizz around windfalls from the peach trees. Her sisters and their men were outside, enjoying the sunset. Dorothy, Hannah, Pete, Danny: they were all so casual, so laid-back. Younger than Finlay and herself, closer to Iris in years and attitude. Dorothy's lack of concern about her boys – Margot could barely get them to eat anything but sugar-rich cereal and ice cream – came close to neglect. And Hannah didn't seem to realise that children needed more sleep than adults: her girls stayed up till all hours watching dreadful stuff on the TV. Margot's sisters just didn't seem to worry the way she and Finlay had done, first with Iris and now with Gayle.

The plans, time, energy – the money too, though they'd never grudged the money – what was the point? With Iris they'd tried to shape their daughter's future just a little, just enough to see her on her way in the world, to avoid making the mistakes she and Finlay had made themselves. But Iris, now they were left holding her baby, while she was God knows where, doing God knows what.

As the last light drained from the sky, the hedgerow chorus swelled. It reminded him of some of the stuff Margot listened to on Radio 3: *Our next piece represents the chaos and disintegration of the twentieth century.* Now playing live in the Devon hedgerows. And on top of all that, from the other side of the seething barricade he could hear a heavy, hollow tread which seemed to keep in time with his own faltering steps. Something was accompanying him, something big. When he stopped, it stopped. Probably a cow or a pony but this closeness, this sweaty intimacy with nature wasn't his cup of tea at all. The sherry was giving him a headache but a headache was preferable to the fingers of panic tightening around his throat.

The darkness was total. He couldn't see the road, was aware of it only through his feet which registered every chip of gravel as a potential danger. He continued, his free hand tapping the air. His invisible companion – which he sincerely hoped was animal rather than human – was clumping along again on the other side of the hedge. Was he walking straight? He had to walk straight or he'd end up in a ditch, scratched to hell. He had to get back, soon, but couldn't hurry; he could only creep, one hesitant step at a time. His sandals made contact with the grass verge. That was it. The verge. He had to stay close to the verge. It was his only way of navigating the suffocating, scented path.

The pain was sudden and appalling, as if he'd pushed

his finger into an electric socket. It jolted up and down his arm repeatedly as the culprit buzzed angrily around him. He bit his throbbing hand, to prevent himself from screaming into the darkness. A wasp, Christ. He flailed forward, for all he knew reeling across the road, intent only on shaking off the bloody thing.

It was only the second time in his life that he'd been stung by a wasp. The first time, oh the first time; at the very end of a very long afternoon picking rosehips to raise money for black babies in Africa. He'd not been at all keen to spend his entire Saturday on the dusty lane which ran round the back of the cemetery. For hours on end he'd dropped bristly hips into a bucket and, to help pass the time, tried to imagine Margot's breasts beneath her sleeveless blouse. Instead of getting his hands on them as reward for his unstinting labour, or any other tangible sign of her interest – a kiss at the very least – a wasp got him on the mouth. Instantly, his lips had ballooned and blistered, turning him into the least desirable boy in 5B.

He'd not been keen but in those early days he'd go out of his way to keep Margot sweet. Ish. Margot was never sweet. Tongue like a lash and a dab hand at slapping and scratching according to all the Duncans, Alecs and Billys she'd knocked back. Good-looking with it, of course, best-looking bird in 4B. Persuading Margot to even consider a date had been a real achievement. And the competition had been part of the attraction.

Now, God help them both, they were so far away from desire. The very word sounded suspect. Margot, of course, had her needs, he did understand that; they'd both been through the mill with Iris and now there was Gayle. Even if they didn't give a toss for each other any more, somebody had to be there to wait until Margot had stopped weeping, blotted her eyes with the heels of her hands and shaken herself back into Capability Jane.

He'd lost all sense of time and direction. Inching his way forward like a blind man, listening hard, all he could hear now was the buzzing hedgerow and his own rasping breath. What had happened to his invisible companion? Why had it deserted him now, left him with nothing to go by but the strip of grass beneath his feet? He'd never wear sandals again; twigs and bits of grit had worked their way between his toes and God knows what nocturnal wildlife might decide to scrabble over his unprotected feet.

The car appeared without any warning. A flood of light pinned him, blinking, in its beam. Before he thought to shout or wave, it was rounding the next corner, the red eyes of the tailplate disappearing. His feet were covered with gravel thrown up by the car as it passed. As he started to walk on, his legs buckled beneath him. If he hadn't been on the verge, that car would have mowed him down.

Dorothy was rubbing aftersun into Pete's shoulders, Hannah and Danny were canoodling on the lounger. Margot didn't mind that everybody else was lazing about, not at all. She wanted everyone to relax, take it easy. It was meant to be a restful family holiday, and she could manage the food perfectly well by herself, in fact preferred total control of the kitchen. If only Gayle would give up whingeing for Finlay. What in God's name was keeping him? He'd just nipped out to replenish the drink – and so he should, he drank enough of it. Had he stopped in the pub again? She'd told him before they came down here that she wasn't going to spend every night as a grass widow, or a pub widow, or any other kind of widow when she had a perfectly capable husband.

She didn't want to think about the other thing but not wanting to think about something was like shining a light on it. Her perfectly capable husband worked too hard, drank too much, only paid attention to his diet when she shoved advice down his throat. Coronary, stroke, ulcer, brain tumour, liver failure, blood clot, the sudden onset of diabetes, epilepsy, catatonia, the names followed each other like a slow cortège from a never-ending war of attrition, the names and their symptoms printed in solid, gloomy type alongside illustrations in her *Family Guide to Health.*

The dinner wouldn't keep much longer. The adults were half-cut and hungry. The children had been fed and left to their own devices but she'd have to try to put Gayle to bed soon. It wouldn't be easy; the child was holding out for Finlay as if her life depended on it. And maybe it did.

He comes upon the driveway without warning and the relief he feels in seeing Margot standing on the lit patio, looking out into the dark, is overwhelming. She's holding the child in her arms – and Gayle is no featherweight – rocking her and looking out, for him maybe, maybe just looking out at the stars. He hurries towards them, walking as straight as he can manage, which isn't very straight at all. Now that he's safe, and can see what he's doing, he's aware that the sherry has taken effect, that he's staggering; but it doesn't matter, nor does his throbbing finger, the main thing is that he's back and Margot is here, with his granddaughter, waiting for him. When he reaches the patio, he raises his empty bottle in greeting. It is the wrong gesture.

Flowers of the Moon

The Six O'Clock Novela

EVENING IN THE hills, just after sunset; fireflies pulse gently in the trees, the air is still hot and hectic with insect activity. On the veranda Kay and Alison are waiting for Hernando, who is down at the pond, pottering.

—It didn't happen here, says Alison. It was at the house in Manguinhos. My place. I've been trying to sell it for ages.

—How could you go on sleeping there?

—No choice. Until I was able to move up here with my old man.

They're already running late, hours late. When Hernando has finished yet another fiddly, last-minute chore he's found for himself, when he's bolted the windows and locked the doors, they pile into his roomy old car which bumps and lurches down the potholed track to the road where they turn, churning up a cloud of dust, and rattle back up to the house. The budgies. They have forgotten the budgies.

To leave the neat, oddly Germanic village of Campinho, they must pass beneath the gatehouse. There isn't a barrier but Kay can imagine one droning down into position, clanking shut, a green light turning red and a squad of athletic, uniformed hoodlums storming out of the orange blossom. But really the gatehouse is very quaint and dinky, a gingerbread cottage on stilts, bedecked with

Christmas lights and sporting a hand-painted banner, in large white letters: SAUDADES.

—It's more than 'Missing you' or 'Haste ye back', says Alison. A great longing, that's what it is, for someone, usually family, dead family, the past. But it's not sad, it's not like your moaning old pibroch.

—Yours too, says Kay.

—Mine too, OK.

—D'you ever miss Scotland?

—Oh aye. All the time, says Alison, laughing.

Alison laughs a lot. The littlest thing tickles her. Living in this hot, noisy country suits her.

—*Saudades* is like a big hug between the living and the dead. I don't think there's a word for it in English. Or a feeling either. Some feelings don't translate.

The budgies are in the back of the car, with Kay, whose job it is to hold them steady as Hernando – a seventy-year-old daredevil – slaloms around bend after hairpin bend with the zest of a boy racer. But then everybody else on the road is driving with a mixture of anarchy and blind faith. From the moment they hit the long winding descent to the city, it's a white-knuckle ride.

—*If I'm to die in a smash, I'd rather be a lemon.* He means he'd rather be an ingredient in the national hooch.

Alison is translating slogans painted on the tailboards of lorries which slash across three lanes at a single wrench of the steering wheel.

—*He who walks barefoot should not plant thistles.*

—*In times of crisis, vultures turn into pheasants.* They're keen on hidden meanings here, says Alison.

—*I know that God is Brazilian but also know He doesn't live here.*

—*I don't have everything I love but I love everything I have.*

—Nice, says Kay. That's nice. A happy man.

—Or a good liar, says Alison.

—*My lorry cuts along the highway. It goes up like inflation and down like the* cruzeiro. He needs to replace *cruzeiro* with *real*, though who knows how long the new currency will last . . .

Kay keeps a tight hold on the budgie cage as much for herself as the birds, which mutter nervously under their flimsy cover, as the car courses towards the scrappy industrial suburbs of Vitória: coffee, chocolate and granite factories, mounds of car tyres and pyramids of watermelons, rows of beat-up storefronts and long, intertwining queues of passengers hoping to board buses which are already packed to far beyond official capacity. Neon motel signs flash on and off in the darkness: KISS, PINK, LOVE GARDEN. *DESCONTO POR TRÊS HORAS.*

—Here, says Alison, a motel is for one thing only: sex. Not just men with their bit on the side; there's plenty of that, loads, but married couples use them too. A private hour or two can be hard to find in an overcrowded country.

Dona Teresa's kitchen is small and full to bursting with women; the overhead fan turns slowly, wearily, as if displacing the scented female air, as if cooling down this lot is too much of an effort. Its whirring is barely heard above the chat, the throaty laughter and clink of crockery as ringed fingers fuss with coffee cups.

The plastic seat covering sticks to the back of Kay's bare knees. She smiles generally and tries to unstick her legs as Alison does the introductions. Kay picks out her own name and where she's from but what's Alison saying which makes these women laugh so much, stretch across the table, plant flowery kisses on her cheeks then settle back into their own frothy conversations?

A thermos flask is pushed across the oilskin tablecloth towards the visitor, the foreign guest. Then a sugar bowl, a crusty loaf on a glass plate, butter melted by the heat into a slick of yellow grease, a dribbling jar of thin, red jam, a long, sharp knife.

Dona Teresa leaves the arms of Hernando, her son, shuffles to the table and nudges the thermos a further few inches until the slim silvery cylinder rattles against Kay's saucer. A small, round woman, freckled like a thrush, leans over and pats Kay's arm.

—Drink, she says. Dona Teresa wants you to drink.

Kay squirts two or three hot black streams of coffee into her cup, adds sugar from a spoon the size of her pinky.

—I am Pilar, says the freckled woman. How are you. I am from Rio de Janeiro.

—Hello Pilar.

—You visit Rio de Janeiro already?

—Not yet.

—When you come, you stay with me. From my kitchen window you can see the very big Christ on the mountain. It is really very big.

Dona Teresa pushes the thermos aside and slides the bread plate over until it, too, rattles insistently.

—Eat, says Pilar. She wants you to eat.

—Aye, says Alison. She won't let you alone until she sees food on your plate.

Kay turns to Dona Teresa.

—Thank you. *Obrigada.*

—Very good!

—*Muito bom!*

—She speaks Portuguese!

Dona Teresa strokes Kay's face and mumbles something unfathomable. Pilar claps and rattles her bracelets. Alison is laughing. It's like being a child again, in a roomful of indulgent mothers. Best keep everybody happy, do as you're told and carve a slice off the fluffy loaf. She spreads runny jam over runny butter and bites into the bread. Dona Teresa, satisfied, inches back into the welcoming arms of her son.

It's the last day of the year and Dona Teresa's is a pit-stop. They're on their way to somewhere else, a beach town with a name full of broad, husky vowels which Kay can't remember. Then on to the other place. A long night ahead.

—So, Kay, how you like Brazil? says Pilar.

—Very much.

Pilar flashes her smile and her earrings, her bracelets and her rings. A heat comes off her, a deep sun-baked heat. She continues in rapid Portuguese. Alison translates.

—Pilar thinks you look sad and Dona Teresa says you're not allowed to be sad in her home.

—No, no. Just tired.

Dog tired; still jet-lagged from the marathon flight, limp as a rag from the stunning heat and maddening insomnia, but New Year must be seen in, one way or another.

—Tired? says Pilar. In Brazil? But we have *café*, cocaine!

—And corruption, says Alison. Don't forget corruption.

—No, don't, says a woman with frizzy black hair. Don't ever forget corruption. She stands up, adjusts the straps of her skimpy sundress and makes her way round the table, hugging and kissing everyone.

—Nana, says Alison, one of Hernando's sisters. The one with the new job and up to high doh about it. The inauguration ceremony is tomorrow. The woman's finally getting a chance to do something, to make a difference and she's cracking up.
Nana doesn't look as if she's cracking up. She looks great.

Pilar, also on her feet now, takes Nana's hands and holds them up.

—This girl, she must have manicure!
The two sixty-year-old women collapse, giggling, into each other's arms, then rush off to find a beauty parlour which is still open.

—Tchau tchau tchau!

—Tchau!

A slight, sullenly pretty girl in a nylon overall comes in from the courtyard and begins to clear away some of the debris.

—Olá Sylvia, says Alison.

The girl nods and hurries off with an armful of dirty crockery.

—Sylvia is Rosa's maid. Rosa needs a lot of help.

Rosa, Hernando's other sister, slopes against Alison and mumbles out of the side of her mouth which works.

—Cheeky old besom, says Alison. She says how come my friend from home doesn't look like me? I look like a milkmaid, she says, whereas you . . . I'm not telling what she says about you. It's far too flattering. Milkmaid indeed! Any more of your cheek, Rosa, and I'll pack you off to your room. Rosa laughs her twisted, cracked laugh and rubs Alison's sturdy pink arm.

Dona Teresa is hovering again. Kay can feel the old woman's wheezy breath on her shoulder. Dona Teresa bends forward, tips the sticky dregs of coffee into the cup of her foreign guest, removes the thermos and wanders off behind the battered Formica cabinet where Sylvia can be heard sloshing dishes around the sink.

Hernando, who has been silently hugging his mother since they arrived, foresees a problem. For the inauguration ceremony, Nana is permitted two guests. Dona Teresa must – as her mother – be one. Tradition would have it that Hernando should be the other guest but Pilar, Nana's lifelong friend, has shown up from Rio. Nana's so wound up about it all that she can't even manage a manicure by herself, never mind a decision. Tomorrow is an important day; the new president will be sworn in and new state officials appointed across the entire country, there will be the possibility of change. TV cameras will be out in force; Nana might even be on the news. Just in case his sister needs him to accompany her, Hernando is in his mother's bedroom, trying on a couple of his dead father's jackets.

—Who the hell is that? says Alison.

A woman is standing in the archway between the kitchen and the interior of the house, an apparition; bootblack hair, scarlet mouth, pearls the size of peas, plunging scarlet vest, long black skirt, patent stiletto-heeled boots.

—God, says Kay. She's like a film star from the fifties.

—You're joking, says Alison. More like a prostitute, no, the ghost of a prostitute. Used to be a *telenovela* where all these ghosts come back to a town and meddle in the lives of the living. Six o'clock *novela*, or the seven o'clock. She'd fit the bill for that part, right enough. Will you look at those pearls!

The light catches the woman's necklace and her pale, outstretched, theatrical arms. Though she is addressing an audience which barely acknowledges her presence, she continues as if the room were hanging on her every word. At the end of her speech she pauses – for applause? – turns and swans off towards the dim interior of the house.

—Bloody hell, says Alison. Inviting us all into the good room. Some people. She doesn't even live here, for God's sake!

Alison puts an arm around Rosa, who does.

—What's going on, Rosa? Tell me about her with the pearls.

Rosa nudges Alison in the ribs and begins to spill the beans. It turns out to be a long and troubling story involving the dispossession of another elderly relation.

—Planning to shove some old dear in a home, nab her house. In the meantime, she's sponging off Rosa and Dona Teresa. Conniving bitch.

It's the time of year for barely remembered relations to turn up uninvited and expect to be accommodated. Dona Teresa doesn't put her foot down any more. She used to, but she's eighty-five now, frail, and her memory's not what it used to be. Nana has become the acting head of the household but Nana works long hours and from tomorrow, will be far too busy rooting out state corruption to sort out home affairs.

—Time to get out of here, says Alison.

* * *

On the small front courtyard, Sylvia, Rosa's maid, is sprawled on the bench beneath her boyfriend; the couple are engaged in lazy, wordless intimacies. A tree laden with flame-red flowers fans out above them. In their holiday home under the stars, the budgies – a father and son who fight and a female who flusters between them – whirr and screech and rattle their cage. Hernando, awkwardly formal now in his dead father's jacket, embraces his mother once more. Dona Teresa straightens her glasses, bolts the high steel gate and steps back into the shadow of the porch. A firecracker gashes the night sky.

Queen of the Sea

IT'S TEN MINUTES to midnight and the traffic hasn't moved more than a car length in half an hour. Horns blast, radios yammer, the smells of bodies, exhaust, blossom, seaweed, charred meat, tobacco, booze and gunpowder waft through the open windows of Hernando's car. A tide of pedestrians floods past, pressing against the car, streaming between queues of stationary vehicles; white-clad pedestrians, white for the queen of the sea.

—It's bloody nonsense like this that causes half the trouble around here, says Alison.

The checkpoint at the entrance to the beach is the cause of the hold-up. Blue-uniformed boys with rifles slung across their shoulders are stopping cars and searching them at random.

—For drugs, says Alison. Guns.

Kay unzips her handbag, rummages inside it until her fingers make contact with the smooth, oily leather of her passport.

—People take guns on the beach? says Kay.

—In Brazil some folk take guns everywhere. Or knives. But tonight – I doubt it. Even muggers and murderers take a holiday.

—This place we're going on to later . . .

—Pedro's. He's having some kind of a party for New Year.

—I mean after that, where we're staying tonight . . . ?

—It was a long time ago.

There's no way the car's going to get them to the beach by twelve and it's in both the women, the need to reach their destination, to arrive, to be there for the bells. The countdown to twelve had to be noted, no matter where you were you couldn't ignore it, the counting out of the old year, the dragging in of the new. No matter how you were feeling this corridor of time had to be travelled through, the rites of passage enacted, for better or worse.

Kay and Alison get out of the car, leaving Hernando to the traffic and the police. Hernando wasn't planning to go to the beach; he still has other social obligations to fulfil. He and Alison kiss through the open car window.

—Tell them whose house you're going to. That'll get you through their stupid roadblock.

They move off along the rutted road, Alison padding along in flip-flops, arms swinging free, easy, unhurried, broad, capable shoulders cutting a path through the crowds. Kay struggles to keep up, trying not to let more than one or two people separate her from her friend, the only person she knows in this swirling foam of people. Sweat streams from her temples, coursing past her ears and down the back of her neck beneath the shirt, borrowed from Alison because she had nothing white for the occasion. A loose well-made shirt, comfortable and sensible, like Alison.

Kay's bag is bothering her; a flimsy cloth handbag, bright green. She holds it close to her body, gripping the soft handles with both hands as if it's full and heavy, as if there's real weight in it: *By law your passport should be with you at all times.* That's what the guidebook said, *at all times.*

And whatever you do, don't fall foul of the police. It wouldn't have been too clever to leave all your documents in a car on New Year's Eve no matter where you were and in a country world-famous for violent crime . . . Instead, she's a mugger's dream; her daft wee bag might as well glow in the dark. Every time a face turns in her direction she flinches, steels herself for a knife-glint in the darkness, a swift slash and all her essential bits of paper whisked out of her hands.

Where the concrete meets the sand, traders have set up a thriving, jangling market of canopied stalls, trestle tables and barrows, selling barbecued meat, corn, beer and *cachaça,* trinkets and lucky charms, cotton hammocks and cassettes of the samba music which is being blasted into their ears.

The dark outstretched arm of sand is starred with people. Their white clothes gleam in the moonlight. White clothes, skin with a treacly sheen, skin the colour of Africa, of slaves shipped and shipped again to this endless coastline, whipped and goaded into cutting roads through the uncharted interior, packed wholesale down the mines, their bones buried beneath gold dust and diamonds.

SwIndia, Hernando said that morning, this country is Switzerland and India in one. A nation of lords and slaves still, of unfettered wealth and unspeakable poverty. Hernando knows about money. A banker would. Hernando knows about inflation and devaluation of currency, credit ratings and national debt, interest and depreciation, asset-stripping and foreign investment – and the crippling lack of it – he knows about all these things.

He began to explain them to Alison's friend from home and she tried to understand. But as she spoke neither the language of the country nor the language of money, it became too confusing for both of them. So, instead, Hernando drew Kay's attention to a hummingbird, whirring down to the plastic-flower feeder which dangled from a tree, poking a proboscis into a plastic stamen and sucking up sugar water. Hernando puts out food for all the wild birds, though there's more than enough food for the taking, more than enough for the birds in the trees.

Drums, chants, firecrackers whizzing from under their feet, squealing past their ears, slamming into the sky, battering the darkness like gunfire. An open-shirted man pours wine over his head; an old, old woman spoons steaming broth into bowls; kids build shadowy sandcastles; throngs of teenage boys follow and are followed by throngs of teenage girls; lovers, fused at the hips, gaze at the sky, a car packed with joyriders gouges a drunken track through the crowds. Thousands, how many thousands have gathered here to stand by the sea?

Across the beach, in dug-out harbours of sand, candles flicker on little reed boats, like Moses baskets. Rings of turbanned, bell-skirted women link arms, sway and make tiny, instinctive leaps into the air, alert to no one but Iemanjá. The queen of the sea is why they are here; offerings must be made. Iemanjá can make the crops grow, bless a new baby, or keep your wife faithful. If she is in the mood. The queen of the sea must be placated.

Firecrackers firecrackers firecrackers firecrackers, the darkness erupting, the sea sand and sky falling in on themselves, the world flattened into flashing silhouettes, black white blue, sky people beach, the sea a white road, the sky a shattered mirror, a face, a glance, a bottle, a mouth, a blurted cheer, a blurred, outstretched arm, breath sweat perfume, booze sugar garlic, close breath, close bodies, the bag pressed to her chest, the precious bloody bag, the sky tipping, the shoreline cracking, a hand, another hand, now, will it happen now, will a hand come out of the dazzling darkness and put a knife to her throat, a gun to her head, that's how it happens, she's seen it on TV, read about it and heard first-hand accounts, will it happen now while the crowds pack closer and closer and the sky's a riot?

Kay presses her face against Alison's arm.

—Christ, if they'd cut out the bangs . . .

—I thought you wanted a bit of local colour! Alison yells in Kay's ear.

—I did. I do, but the noise!

—We don't have quiet celebrations around here! Happy New Year!

—Happy New Year!

—It's great to have you here! Never thought you'd make it!

Hugs, kisses, firecrackers, firecrackers. Kay puts her hands over her ears and shuts her eyes. She's made it all the way here but will she make it through the New Year?

—Will you look after me, Alison?

—For God's sake. And you were always the adventurous one. Always the wanderer. You came for a change, didn't you, something different?

—I know, I know.

—Might as well take a look around you, then.

—I can't. I can't look. I'm scared.

—What? I can't hear you!

—I'm scared, Alison.

—Of what?

—I don't know. Everything. The crowds, the bangs.

—For God's sake!

Alison laughs, as usual.

A prolonged battery of firecrackers arcs towards the sea, fountains of flame dripping from their tails. Kay clings to her friend's arm, lets herself be led like a child to the shore where columns of entranced women, holding aloft the little boats, sway through petticoats of foam into the waves, the weight of wet cloth dragging them down. When they are waist-deep, their skirts float to the surface and spread out, pale blooms on the dark water. The boats are launched; they dip and toss, the candle light marking out their paths across the dark immensity of water.

—It's bad luck if a boat comes back, says Alison. It means Iemanjá has rejected the offering. Doesn't fancy the cheap wine, maybe. Or prefers fresh flowers to plastic. Or just happens to be in a mean mood . . . Pretty, isn't it?

—Yes. Beautiful. But . . . but could we go now?

They've not been on the beach long, hardly any time at all, and it's really amazing and beautiful, and everyone's enjoying themselves, not a mean look on a single face, not a drunken rammy in sight, it's a spectacle Kay might never see again in her whole life, this beach at midnight, thousands united in celebration . . .

—The bangs, the crowds, this bloody bag. I've got the lot here, Alison. Passport, cheques, plane ticket. Didn't know what else to do with them.

—For God's sake. Now she tells me.

—It's around here somewhere. A blue door, we're looking for a blue door. A fancy one, as I remember. This might be the way.

It isn't. At the far end of the street, a foggy yellow lamp struggles to illuminate a tiny patch of ground. The houses are shuttered and dark; thick-leaved trees overhang trellised walls. Their footsteps ring out in the heavy still air, still enough for Kay to hear her heart exploding and exploding.

—It's definitely around here somewhere, says Alison. Feeling any better yet?

—I will in a minute.

But how much more of this silent darkness before they find the place where Hernando is supposed to be and they can sit down and drink something, something cold, anything to wash away the barb of panic twisting in her throat?

As they walk on slowly, Kay's foot hits something on the pavement, something soft but solid. A hand stretches up from the darkness, a small dusty hand holding out three packets of chewing gum. A hand and then the face of a crop-headed, half-naked boy, no more than six or seven and as thin as the plastic bag on which he's been sleeping. His eyes are open but his gaze is cloudy, unfocussed.

—Chiclet. Chiclet.

The high, frail voice, the exhausted eyes.

—Christ, says Kay. I kicked him. Can you tell him I'm sorry?

—I suppose so. He'll not expect an apology.

—Tell him anyway. Please.

Alison hikes up her skirt, squats on the dusty pavement beside the boy and says something much longer than *My friend says she's sorry she kicked you* in any language. Whatever it was that she said, it makes him laugh, rub the sleep out of his eyes and try again for a sale.

—How much does he want for the gum? says Kay.

—Too much, says Alison. One *real* each. Double the usual price.

Kay unzips her bag, slips a five from her purse and hands it to the boy. The boy gives her all three packets of gum and rummages in the pockets of his ragged shorts.

—He won't have change, says Alison. They never do.

—It doesn't matter. Tell him it doesn't matter.

—But it's too much. You're giving him too much. He'll turn into a thief, if he isn't one already.

—It's New Year, says Kay. It's nothing.

Alison shakes her head, and gives the boy a protracted explanation of her foreign friend's misguided generosity. Again the boy's frail laughter peals into the dark, still air. Smiling widely, he secretes the money in his only item of clothing, scratches his dusty head and beds down again on his plastic sheet.

—*Obrigado,* says the boy. *Feliz ano novo.*

Zipping up her bag, Kay follows Alison around the corner, taking care where she puts her feet.

—Now that, says Alison, was dangerous. The Chiclet kid could have had a gang of big bad brothers behind the wall.

—He looked so young.

—He is. Young, desperate, capable of anything. Has to be, or he'd be dead.

The street they've turned into is better lit than the previous one and lined with high walls spiked with broken glass. A car pulls up and stops. Two women in evening dress slide out and pass through an open door, from which escape slender, sparkling threads of music, laughter.

—I think we're here, says Alison. Are you up for this?

—I don't know, says Kay, I don't know.

Rhinewein

—BLOODY HELL, SAYS Alison. The doorman's better dressed than we are.

They shake the remaining traces of beach out of their sandals before making their way to a table on the edge of the lawn. Seeing them approaching, Hernando raises his glass and beams.

—A posh do, says Alison. My old man knows some fancy folk through the bank. We don't have to stay long.

Silver salvers, ice-buckets, frosty blue bottles of chilled Rhinewein. Hugs, kisses, bright smiles and a fleeting once-over from the hostess.

—*Feliz ano novo*! Welcome to Brazil. I am Dolores. I don't speak English.

Dolores, her bronze dress shimmering as she walks, leads Kay and Alison to the kitchen where two tailcoated waiters, skewers and carving knives at the ready, stand to attention at the laden granite table. It's another world from Dona Teresa's cosy overcrowded kitchen: gleaming tiles from floor to high ceiling, polished wood and brass, masses of unoccupied space. Dolores gives them a swift tour of the feast, tapping each plate of meat with a fingernail which perfectly matches her dress.

—Wild boar, Alison translates, not just plain old pig. Pedro, our host, shot it on his estate.

A waiter points to some tiny balls of lead shot nestling on a lettuce leaf.

—The turkey's also from the estate.

—Did Pedro wring its neck? Kay whispers.

—Don't ask, says Alison. Dolores says eat what you like and welcome to her home.

—*Obrigada. Muito obrigada.*

Here you go again. Thank you, thank you. Much obliged. You don't want to be obliged but you are and grateful to be in a place where you can safely dump your handbag on the table and expect it to be there when you get back.

—Hungry?

—Don't know. Probably.

—Then eat. Your jammy piece at Dona Teresa's wasn't much to be going on with.

But it had been good at the crumb-strewn table, comforting, to be sat among grannies and aunties, mothers and sisters, their soft bare arms and flimsy blouses, flowery scents and deep dark lipsticks; a conspiracy of women, their confetti of conversation whirling beneath the cranky old fan.

—How the other five per cent lives, says Alison.

They take their plates and return to their table. Hernando has been joined by a middle-aged man in crisp shorts and open-necked shirt.

—Pedro, says Alison. You don't want to get into conversation with him. Hernando talks money with him – fine – but when our host gets on to humanity, he's none too liberal.

Pedro: sleek, glossy hair matches his spotless, all-white party gear. He is smoking a cigarette through a slim black holder, narrowing his eyes as he inhales. Hernando asks for some of the blue-bottled wine which has been doing the rounds. The waiter makes a discreet little detour to confer with Pedro.

—Must be the good stuff, says Alison.

When the waiter returns with a frosty bottle, he pours each of them a modest half-glass, twirls the bottle to catch stray drips and whisks it off the table. Hernando lays a gentle hand on his arm. After another wordless confab with Pedro, the bottle is left on their table. Hernando's old eyes twinkle with boyish glee.

—Chancer, says Alison. These days, he's content with small victories. Wasn't always. Used to make trouble for people. Pedro included. Tried to make folk do things properly, without greasing palms here, there and everywhere. You're not listening.

—I am, I am.

—You're miles away. Nostalgic for falling about in the snow?

—The slush, as I remember. No, not homesick; just adjusting. Trying to.

—Remember the Swedes who lived across the landing from me?

—Didn't know them as well as you.

—I don't think anybody did.

—You couldn't decide which of them you wanted.

—Oh, I knew all right, says Alison. Jörgen. Made a total idiot of myself one New Year, flaked out in a tear-stained heap on the landing. Still, Lars rolled home from some disco, having failed to get himself a lumber and there on his doorstep was *An Available Woman.*

—Lars? Why did I think of Per?

—That was another night. And Cristof another. Every

one of them got their bed and breakfast across the landing except the one I wanted. Typical.

—It was a long time ago.

—Don't remind me. Twenty years.

—More.

—All right! Couldn't be doing with it now. Too complicated. A laugh at the time, when it wasn't pure bloody hell. That Jörgen had me twisted round his big Nordic toe.

—Don't think I ever met him, says Kay.

—I wish he'd been a bastard but he wasn't. Jörgen was Mr Nice, Mr Level-headed, Not-interested Nice. Saving himself for some woman at home. Admirable, of course, says Alison.

—Now who's nostalgic?

—Not me.

—No *saudades*? says Kay. No great longings?

—Nah, says Alison. Wee ones maybe.

Hernando has taken off his dead father's jacket and hung it carefully over the back of his seat. It is heavy linen, ash-grey, a well-cut jacket, made to last longer than a lifetime. He winks at Kay, puts his arm around Alison and squeezes her appreciatively. Over the years, Alison has rounded out, ripened like a peach.

—My old man likes fat women. Suits me.

She snuggles up to Hernando; he squeezes some more.

—Rhinewein, says Hernando, refilling their glasses.

—Just as well he can't follow our conversation. Hell of a jealous, so he is.

Pedro blows a narrow funnel of smoke across the table. Kay can smell his cologne, a tart, physical scent; it's altering the taste of her food, turning it sour and sharp in her throat. The humid air thumbs her eyes, her temples.

—Pedro wants to know if you like the wild boar, says Alison.

—Very nice. Delicious.

—A six-monther, he says it was, a piglet, reared specially for New Year. And the little chickens are just twenty-four days old.

—*Primera canção,* says Hernando. First song.

—Pedro says young meat is the sweetest.

Kay looks down at her plate and sees infanticide.

—He wants to know if you go hunting in Scotland.

—Never, says Kay.

Pedro stubs his half-smoked cigarette in the ashtray, shakes hands with Hernando, rises and goes to join another table on the lawn, occupied by a pair of wafer-thin blondes.

—Something else, aren't they, says Alison, following Kay's gaze. Pedro's daughters.

—They don't look real.

—Well, if it wasn't exactly what nature gave them, the plastic surgeon did a good job.

—The legs. That tan. Look like they've been lying on the beach for months.

—They probably have.

When the blue bottle is finished, Hernando tries for another but after much toing and froing on the part of the waiter, he's told that the Rhinewein is finished which, for Hernando, is reason enough to leave. Kay, too, is ready to go, more than ready. But not at all happy about the farewell ritual.

—Everyone?

—It's the custom. When in Brazil . . .

—But I haven't even spoken to most of them.

—I bet you've kissed plenty strangers at home. And not just at New Year.

—Maybe, but this is different.

—Of course it's bloody different. Did you want it to be the same? Just do it, will you, and we can get out of here.

—Couldn't I just meet you at the door?

—For God's sake.

Kay picks up her bag, takes a deep breath and follows Alison and Hernando as they meander from one table to another, follows them through one protracted embrace after another. The earrings of strangers swing against her neck, the hair of strangers brushes her own, the lips of strangers alight on her cheek like insects; warm skin, cool skin, smooth skin, stubble. Pedro last. Standing squarely on his flawless lawn, eyes steady and level with hers, arms closing around her shoulders, the narrow, cold smile dissolving into a blur as their cheeks touch, as his breath burns her ear . . . his cologne, his suffocating cologne . . . The smell of him clings to her as she hurries to the doorway where the hired help are still standing to attention.

—You don't have to kiss *them*, says Alison, laughing as usual.

In the car Kay asks,

—Is Pedro German?

—Possibly. You can never be sure.

Earlier in the evening, so much earlier, when they'd been driving through the village in the hills, they'd passed an open-air Lutheran mission, its pews lined with flax-haired blue-eyed settlers, families who'd been there for generations, working the land, building their neat, wood-panelled homes. Without the palms and samba music, the village might have been in Bavaria. And what of the other blond blue-eyed immigrants who came from Europe under cover of night? Were they, too, holed up in the hills on sprawling estates with wild boar for the shooting and fat turkeys for the strangling, those others with new names, new identities, new careers in politics, commerce, law and order?

—Here we are, says Alison. Manguinhos. My place.
Across the driveway, a huge cactus covered with swollen, creamy buds, big as fists, thrusts up into the darkness.

—Flowers of the moon, says Alison. They bloom in the dark, close up in daylight. Spectacular but so short-lived. Two or three nights of glory before they blacken and fall to the ground.

Slowly they climb the creaking wooden stairs. Insects buzz and scuttle as Alison opens her door to the sweet, insidious smell of rot and damp, of the climate taking over. The rusty strings of her old piano twang in time to their footsteps as they clump up another flight of stairs. In the living area, chunks of driftwood prop up bookshelves lined with familiar titles, textbooks from their shared student days; commentaries, essays and modern classics. The climate has been wholehearted in its attack on this body of knowledge; Alison's books are turning into fungal creatures, spores of mould furring the covers, rashes of mildew speckling the pages.

Hernando holds his dead father's jacket at arm's length, and talks to it. Alison translates.

—He says: *He may or may not wear the jacket to his sister's inauguration. He may or may not attend the ceremony but will certainly watch the TV broadcast of the new president being sworn in.* In other words, he'll be glued to the box all day.

—He says: *His sister's appointment is also important. It will be good and not so good.* Very illuminating, Hernando.

—He says: *There are so many connections now, so many links. For example, Dolores, Pedro's wife, should be charged with corruption. Nana, Hernando's sister, will be responsible for instigating procedures.* For God's sake Hernando, so formal. She'll be digging the dirt. That's what she's there for. Looks like we won't be on Pedro's guest list next year.

Hernando hangs the jacket on a wall hook and begins to draw a series of bolts across the door which divides the sleeping area from the rest of the house. Alison tosses Kay a sheet and pillowcase.

—You're in there. Lock your room door, too. And try to get some sleep.

A narrow, child-size bunk, a teddy bear, its face half-eaten by moths, a wooden boat with a mottled sail. A scrap of curtain flaps at the grilled, open window. Outside, a dog howls, a woman laughs and cries and laughs again, dry branches snap and crack in the restless breeze. The moon dips into cloud. Inside, when the howls and laughter have subsided, Kay can hear an unmistakable scratching in the rafters. Tonight Alison's son is in Rio de Janeiro, and Kay is lying on his mattress, horribly wide awake.

This is where it happened, in the dead of night, her friend waking to the hissing whisper of a stranger at her bedside and the stunned, frozen face of her six-year-old son, a gun at his head, the barrel embedded in his curls. And another man, another gun, Hernando dragged out of bed, his old head shoved against Alison's which is shoved against the bedroom wall. A voice asking over and over where they keep their jewels, their cash. Nobody keeps their money in the bank any more, not even a banker, so where's the stash? They've already searched the house and found nothing at all worth taking but there can't be nothing, this is a big house, Hernando's a big man, they know who they're dealing with; a man who lunches with Pedro and his pals must have something to steal. The other voice butting in, talking about saving bullets, a scared, panicky voice saying one bullet is all they're worth, one bullet would go through both skulls, no problem at this range, let's do it and get the hell out . . .

It was a long time ago; miraculously, they are all still alive.

[illegible] either, [illegible] shooting [illegible] to the [illegible] out of [illegible] against the [illegible] with a [illegible] where they keep the [illegible] each. Nobody [illegible] money [illegible] anyway [illegible] banker [illegible] already [illegible] and found nothing [illegible] what [illegible] part [illegible] be nothing [illegible] they know who [illegible] Pedro and his [illegible] must have something [illegible] The [illegible] young [illegible] a [illegible]

It [illegible] they are all still alive.

War Dolls

OSWALDO IS LATE. Maybe he forget how quick the jungle grow; it creep up while the back is turn, the eyes is close. Me, I no sleep good. Some nights, no sleep at all. Always is possible Angél show up but Angél is *nada.* Is no from fear I lie in the dark and listen to bugs and dogs, the scrip-scrip of geckos, the soldiers' boots. People say I have no fear.

Angél no agree but Angél no here. Angél have other things to do than wait in this boxroom above the *zapatería,* breathing in the stink of leather and burnt rubber, crazy from the smell and all day the tap-tap of the hammer. Angél, he away, always away. He make plans, I know he make plans for a better life but me, I sit on my ass, wait for Oswaldo and wonder why he no come.

Long time ago, when we was kids, was the other way round; Oswaldo staying, me going, me coming back with apologies or gifts or nothing but a kick in the pants. One day you go, amigo, but we, we still be here, with the soldiers' guns ready for us, the soldiers' hungry eyes following our girls.

My people wait too long. The map of their waiting is drawn deep into the skin; faces like dry riverbeds, eyes without interest or hope. In the plaza everywhere you can see the same look in the eyes. You people, I think you find it . . . convenient. The sun throw light on white shirts, black hats and slow, sick eyes – dramatic, no? And of course the military, the military is another take.

Is impossible to describe to you this pain of waiting. You see poverty, disease, death – of course, is all here, looking back at you. Accusing. And you, with the expensive camera, are you thinking about the soundtrack? Are you trying to decide which tune from your collection of world music is best with this *foto* tragedy – some mountain flutes, some *canciones de los poetas revueltas*, or maybe better, as contrast, some drunk and crazy *mariachi* . . . Or maybe no music, maybe you let the moving pictures speak for theyself?

I have my own ideas. I too plan to make a film about this situation. You see, I know you will take these little bits of me talking – and maybe Oswaldo, maybe even Angél if you lucky – and twist them into a story but your story, amigo, is only a scratching in the dust. A puff of wind, the whisper of trouble some other place and it will blow away. Your story no good. I no sit here sick with worry for Oswaldo only so you can piss on me.

You want Oswaldo to take you to Angél. You want me to help you do this. People say our leader is *recluso.* Also that he has beautiful girlfriends and many important international contacts. They say he like late-night parties but also early mornings in meditation and the study of philosophy. Believe what you like. Maybe all true. But no important. Our leader is *nada.* I only half year in school but I see and I think, fuck. My people still waiting; on every street in every town. Look outside – I am fortunate to have a window – so many poor people, like me and Oswaldo, be born, grow up and die on the street, in public.

You want Angél be star of your movie, me I want

Oswaldo. That boy; I want make film of he, in the mask and balaclava, eyes straight to camera, voice fuzzy because of the mask, a toy M16 in his hands. No joke, amigo. Is never enough real guns for everybody but can do much with wood and shoe polish. Is no too much problem for Oswaldo. Oswaldo a smart bastard. Me too, eh? Well, me and Oswaldo, we still alive.

Emilia is also in this town now, but alive? *No sé.* Maybe you go find her in the plaza, look and decide for youself. When Oswaldo and me was kids, if we no get money from gringos, Emilia, she kick us out the bus station like dogs. Then, Emilia have good job, sitting behind window of ticket booth; taking money and giving tickets. Then, Emilia young and pretty. She have eyes for Angél and Angél, he make promise he no can keep. America. *Téjas.* The same promise everybody make, same made-up story, same lie, amigo. But people believe what they want and now Emilia she all day in the plaza with the other mothers, sewing, sewing, sewing; no eyes for nothing but pesos and war dolls, pesos and war dolls.

How to find Emilia? No so easy, maybe. So many like she, head turn from the sun, back bent, busy making doll smaller than a match, hands quick as fish but the eyes; look in the eyes. I tell you for nothing, Emilia no so old as she look, no the wise *vieja* you people like put in *documental.* Maybe to you she look like she already live a long and interesting life but Emilia only thirty-five years. And now Angél no have eyes for she, Emilia's life is *nada.* Remember, amigo, if you find she, remember when you pick up a little stick soldier, say the price too high and put it down.

Eh, even the air is slow and heavy from waiting for change. You see the way the dust hang over the square like sorrow and the leaves on the trees droop like dead men's fingers? The soldiers is bored, bad-tempered. This week, they shoot many many dogs; Emilia, she fear for her daughter. Never I like this town. Too high up, too many churches. You visit the churches already; you see all the gold inside? Eh, make me crazy. And too quiet. When I was kid I come here one time, to steal for Angél.

Now I wait for Oswaldo. Maybe wait all night and Oswaldo no show. You know, amigo, I think Oswaldo not too far away. But even if he come tonight, maybe he no speak, to me, to you, to nobody. Maybe nothing to say. Wait and hope is all. Soon is darkness. If you want sleep in hotel bed, go now. For soldiers, curfew is time for badness. Soldiers too is poor kids; killing work put food in the belly and boots on the feet.

In my head I see Oswaldo's death many times; so many ways to die. And if Oswaldo no come back, I alone. *Sí*, I have the compadres, I live for they but sometimes I feel too much alone, too far away; the compadres is not enough. This boy. I no sleep because when I close the eyes, I see Oswaldo die, and me, I see me filming the death of this brave and foolish boy. I see my people waiting so long only newsreel left; the dead total flash on screen, mothers scream for bleeding *niños*. But no sound; only voiceover story. No real screaming on the news. And me, I see me fall down dead in the dust, like movie cowboy, still holding a camera, still making movie. Or the only one alive, only one still walking, walking across the plaza; the ground red, shadows crawling over the dead as *los cóndores* come down from the sky in a slow black spiral and I no can stop looking, I keep filming, because no one else is left to see. Eh, but this happens when you wait too long, you imagine the worst things.

All day I have this pain like a toothache, like my mouth is shoe-leather and somebody hammering nails in. Maybe it's just the stink of *huaraches* or the heavy air, maybe no more than that. But we have always been close, Oswaldo and me, and sometimes we know things about each other without speaking. Is not so crazy, amigo, to feel pain when someone you love is hurting.

Eh, this talking is thirsty business. No water; Coca and Fanta only. Warm fizzy shit. It blow up the belly and rot the teeth but what else to wash dust from the mouth? Beer, tequila? Sometimes I want drink, drink until the walls spin and sleep come quick as a kiss but for me, no drink, drugs. And no women. People say Angél come a long way but really he is like always, he push people around. One time Oswaldo and me, we steal and sell the skin for Angél. Now, for Angél and the people, maybe we die.

To die no problem. I tell you already, people say I have no fear. Maybe is true. Only, the movie. I no make my movie. Eh, you talking to one dumb *chico,* no? One more loco think he can change this world when he heading *rápido* for the next. In the next world, no Coca and no Angél. Or else I also quit that place. But you no interest, eh, no interest in Oswaldo, Emilia, me. We nothing special, eh, nothing special. Is Angél you want on film; mystery man.

Is smart to take it easy, amigo. All this up and down to the window like you waiting on a girl. Rest the feet; maybe you need the feet *rápido.* Sit. Drink a fucking Fanta. Count geckos on the wall. You no like the smell from downstair? You want your hotel room? If no go now, you miss dinner – Emilia's daughter carrying big tourist plate of meat, beans, rice. You see this girl already, eh, the beautiful Angelina? Touch her, amigo, I feed your balls to the dogs.

So; you and me till dawn? You, me and five hundred pairs of *huaraches*. I think it will be a long night. In the night, time grow like the jungle. In this town, even before the soldiers, is quiet here, so quiet, any sound at all can stop the breath, if you have fear. And you, I can see you have plenty fear, amigo. Not in the eyes – you know to make the eyes steady – but on the mouth I see a little twitch. Fear make you hold on to life.

Me, maybe I no want hold on. Is cold, eh? Feel the walls. Is like inside a cave, wet and cold. This place, eh, this town above the clouds. I come here first when I eleven years. The bus it drive right through the clouds and keep going. I think maybe we drive to heaven. Funny, amigo, eh? Then, I no want go to heaven, only *Téjas*. This *gringa* in the bus station, she say maybe *Téjas*, maybe. She like me. I hope and hope. I smile. *Nada*. Only this place. Maybe, if she had take me to *Téjas*, I be president of USA by now, or big movie-maker, driving three days non-stop in my Cherokee Trailblazer back to my home – only here is no my home and no my people, no really – I have only Oswaldo.

You hear boys whisper *Téjas, Mister, Téjas*, in your ear, you still hear them? How you shake off the smiling boys, who drift around the bars like smoke? And your *documental*, how it help they? No your problem, eh? Your problem is how many days, how many dollars. You buy your *información*, your story, get out. Because if you wait, fear grow inside, creeping and choking. Is when you begin to feel naked, when the breath burn cold in the throat and you dream of home, your girl. Is when you go to the bar for American beer, American whiskey and wonder if our girls is worth the risk . . . Eh, amigo, you have standards, I know. But standards like road signs, they change with the road. On a big highway the signs are bright, see easy. On a little road some signs is eat up by jungle, fade from sun. The path Oswaldo must take have no sign.

How to pass the hours? Maybe you tell me about your life, home, your girl. You have a girl, yes? Tell me about your girl. No problem, amigo, is just for me something to put in the head, a picture to put in the head. And why not a picture of your girl? Tell me, is she blonde, blue-eyed? I like to think about this girl. What she do when she happy to see you? I been here a long time, a man must do something to pass the time. I tell you already, no women for me. Is better I am alone but desire no rest, amigo, desire has no walls, checkpoints, is free to go where it want, to climb into Angelina's bed and breathe in the smell of her warm, oiled hair, eh, the beautiful Angelina.

So, when you no make *documental*, you do home movies? You shoot your girl being sexy? She like do dirty things for camera? No? She no like, or you no like say? What girl like a man who chase other people's pain? You know they say a man alone is *poco loco*, and a loco with a gun . . . my gun is no toy, amigo. Is better to keep happy a man with a gun, no? Show me your camera. Let me hold it in my hands, amigo, look through the lens . . . Good quality, very good. *Muchos dólares* for this camera, no? More than a gun. More than two, three guns, maybe. Be careful where you go. Somebody maybe try to steal it from you. Very good. I can see all the way to the plaza.

But tell me about your girl. You think about she when you lie in your hotel bed? If no go now, amigo, no bed for you tonight, only little broke chair. Unless you want lie with me?

When Angél come here – only one time – he no like. Too small, smelly, too dusty. He cough, cough. Is the land here – dry, dry. In America, good land, plenty land, fields so big you no see the end. Angél always he think big. But here is small people, small farms, fields like bed sheets spread out to dry. Angél have big ideas but me, sometimes now I think pesos in the hand better than bodies in the street. But if Oswaldo take off his mask, put down his toy gun, will gringos buy Emilia's dolls? If no war, what will Emilia sell?

Before the fighting, the women make trouble dolls, tiny tiny, for help *niños* sleep. Little bit magic, eh? You tell trouble to doll, the doll take away. But now, too many troubles, maybe only guns and *documentales* can fix things. Listen; it begin already. You no hear nothing? Your ears is block? You no hear the dog cry and the clock-clock, like chopping wood . . . eh, but is no dog, is girl; the soldiers take a girl. Better she die now, before they put her in truck. You ever see cat catch mouse? It catch, it let go, catch again, throw in the air before it bite off the head. Even after the mouse no can crawl, no can squeak, the cat play. The girl is mouse for the soldiers. To know and do nothing is terrible, terrible. If I no wait for Oswaldo, my only friend, I say fuck Angél's orders, fuck the big plans.

You hear now eh, you hear now? I think is big mistake for you to stay here, tonight. This no safe house. Me, I stay and cry for this girl and hope Angél has good plans. You, I think you must go now. But the camera is problem.

Soldiers, they no like *documentales.* They see camera after curfew, maybe you road kill. Must be very careful, very quick. Maybe hotel door already close, *no sé,* but listen, I make deal. You give me camera, I give you gun. My gun no toy, amigo. Also plenty ammo, see? Is time to leave your story, eh? So give, take, go.

A Day Without Dancing

Every day I count wasted in which
there has been no dancing

Nietzsche

THE COURTYARD HAS a way of catching voices and flinging them around, of magnifying every sound so, though it's a quiet place – some days as quiet as the village graveyard with its proliferation of glazed, everlasting flowers – if people are around, I know about it. Inside the L-shaped building where I wait for my night visitors, sounds roll down the wood-floored corridors: boot heels, keys scraping in locks, coughs. It's as well that the apartments have been modernised and the beds are plain, new creaky affairs from the IKEA outside Paris. I wouldn't want the history of this place crawling out of my mattress; better it skittles in from a corridor or drifts through the open window and its pale leaf-printed curtains, mirroring the garden.

All the occupied apartments and studios look inwards on to the courtyard, giving the impression that the artists prefer to huddle together, to look out at each other or down the long slim garden to the river and turn their backs on the sleepy village. But it would be unfair to say that the locale is of no interest to them – every day they make their forays into the outside world; they shop for bread, meat, stamps, wine and drop into the Hotel de la Terrasse to drink coffee, cognac, pastis, to hear French spoken and put aside the tongues they have brought with them. And when the quaint delights of the village are exhausted, there are plenty of walks, most of which involve the river or the canal.

The roads are to be avoided; for such a rural place the traffic is heavy and hostile to pedestrians. This wasn't so when my night visitors were physically in residence. No cars and motorbikes then, no woodcutters with chainsaws tearing holes in tranquil afternoons, just horses clopping around and carriage wheels trundling over cobbles. Armed with notebooks and palettes, the writers recorded walks in the forest, the painters propped up easels all over the place and reinvented the river, the willows and wash-houses, the mill, and – endlessly – each other.

Nowadays the artists might as well be on the moon; the landscape and those who inhabit it rarely feature in anybody's work. I'm aware that depicting the picturesque has been passé for several generations but to wilfully ignore one's surroundings, is it not wasteful? I try not to pry but sometimes I wonder what this lot do with their time. And my suggestions. I'm beginning to think they don't hear anything I say, or have decided to ignore me. I know this is nonsense, a muse must carry on for eternity, available to all comers, but I can't help hoping that I might be able to retire. Sometimes I forget that they are here at all, sometimes I imagine no living person is here, that I'm alone in the building with only my night visitors for company.

August (Mr Strindberg) is with me now. I need my wits about me when August appears. He was always hard work but now . . . He shows me a photograph, of Verlaine on his deathbed. The poet's body is propped up on pillows, face turned to the wall, a spray of flowers at the head and feet.

—You see the animal, big animal, on Verlaine's stomach?

August's eyes are glassy.

—What kind of animal?

—Ach! Questions! Animal, big animal, there. And there, on the floor, little . . . *djavül* . . .

The photograph is very old and faded. I hold it under my swan-necked IKEA bed light and look again; the floral wallpaper in the background looks dusty and indistinct, the pattern disappearing in places but there's no animal or *djavül*; August is hallucinating. Among other things, he has become infected by the fashion for dabbling in alchemy. If only he would turn his face to the sun instead of glowering into darkness all the time, he would have no need for such nonsense. He's clean, well dressed, attractive in an intense kind of way but so gloomy. I wish I knew some good jokes. Gloomy visitors have a way of making me feel too responsible for them, unlike cheery ones. August's gloom hangs over me like a punishment.

—Why don't you go up to Paris, I say. Enjoy yourself for a change.

—Paris! Temptations! Too many temptations!

Everything here smells of anise; the detergent, the washing-up liquid, the furniture polish, the sweets in their pretty tins, the drink, the food. It's pleasant at first but over-powering, eclipsing everything else; a bit like August, who is at the window, smoking as always, looking out into the courtyard and scowling. Tonight the artists are sitting out on the patio, eating and drinking. It's a mild night; the spring breeze carries the tang of sap and bonhomie. The candles twitch faintly, faces around the table bloom as the yellow light flows over them.

—This sitting around, talking, this discussing, for what?

—They're having a party, August. Ramon's wife Ritta has just arrived from Spain.

—Madrid or Barcelona?

—I don't know. It's a welcome party.

—Welcome! For what she come?

—To be with Ramon, I suppose. To stop him being lonely.

—Nobody stop lonely. No wife, no husband stop lonely.

—Perhaps it's nicer being lonely together.

—Lonely always hell. Always, always hell.

August's line in conversation could wear down anyone's spirit, even that of a seasoned muse like myself. But even though he was glaring down at the welcome party for Ritta, he was interested all the same.

—Why he sit like stone? Why no dance?

—Nobody else is dancing.

—But his wife she come.

—Yes . . . Did you ever dance, August?

—In dreams only. My wife she dance. My wife make me lonely.

I expect August's wife has been making a bit too much of an impression. She's a striking woman who thrives on attention and – being an actress – knows how to get it. If August won't listen to me, a woman who keeps him on his toes is a good thing. And if she makes him greedy for her glances, too bad.

—Were you a good dancer in your dreams?

—I don't remember. But you see this little wife of Ramon, she so happy, throwing her smile to everybody. But he, he look at his feet. You see, you see this?

—I see nothing from my bed.

—You get up. You look.

—I've seen her already, August. She seems nice.

—Nice. Nice! What is this nice?

August is right about the dancing. More dancing is what this place needs. Peace is an airy thing but the silence which hangs over the tiled patio and its primrose-yellow coach lights is heavy, suffocating as smog. My night visitors had little time for silence. Of course they spent some of their time with no one but me whispering in their ears but otherwise they ate and drank and talked, sucked the juices and chewed the bones of each day as if it were their last. And I am right about August; he's drawn to Ramon's wife exactly because – like his own wife – she doesn't save her personality for the conjugal bedroom.

Perhaps August sees himself in Ramon. Ramon has been on a ten-day bender. A friendly and philosophical drunk, he tacked in and out of the Hotel de la Terrasse declaring that he'd solved the problem of existence, found the key to life in the swaying bright sail of alcohol. He sobered up only just in time for his wife's arrival. Everybody knew about Ramon's drinking; he stopped the others in the street to tell them about it. But now his wife is here and he's better; subdued, withdrawn, but better. As soon as Ritta arrived, they had sex, to reggae music. Accompanied by Toots and the Maytals a few moans of pleasure filtered into the courtyard. I expect they'll be at it again later, making up for lost time.

Edvard's wife isn't due to arrive for some weeks yet but Edvard is a more self-sufficient man, tidy as a well-tended allotment, amusing himself – and occasionally others – with esoteric jokes. Of them all, Edvard has most faith in me. In his quiet, meditative way he has been reducing the world to what he sees are its essentials; coloured rings in grey, blue and orange, the colour scheme of the centre. There is a part of Edvard's imagination which he conceals even from me, possibly the most interesting part. It is linked to an earlier period in his life, to the songs of Jacques Brel and Edith Piaf.

Jan is missing his wife badly. Though she writes every day, he moons about his room, agonising about whether his opera about the fall of the Berlin Wall will ever be completed. Self-doubt and the weight of the past press on Jan's rounded shoulders and if, during his inspirational walks, he must cross paths with any of the others, he becomes hunched and anxious as a fugitive. Like Ramon, I think he too may be more fond of the bottle than of me.

August is really more interested in the wider picture and is pleased to discover that in the village at least, things haven't changed much. The old wash-houses on the riverbank are still there, though now they shelter small boats or have become weekend picnic huts for folk from the city. The villagers are still squat blocks of humanity who move slowly, talk fast and put on white shirts for Sunday. The café clientele lurches from one inebriated generation to another and the butcher's wife is still a pink, fleshy woman with muscular legs, dainty feet and a trilling, metallic *bonjour*. On the medieval bridge, in the afternoon sun, old men and children throw bread to the river birds and young men, caps pulled low over their eyes, pretend to fish. August wants to know if there are still coypu in the river. There are; at night they swim beneath the bridge, noiseless black blurs which barely ripple the water. Satisfied, August nods and departs.

Laughter rises from the patio. Edvard has told a joke which for once everybody understands. Even Ramon is laughing, his deep voice creaking like a wheelbarrow. The meal is finished and the cleaning up, or, as August has it, *the interminable toil of keeping life's dirt at bay*, has begun. There is a great deal of cleaning done here. Sweeping and soaping, sponging and mopping; in this they work as a team, a busy, efficient, wholehearted team. If only they could approach their art so clearly, cleanly.

—You are resting again, you lazy girl!

I always feel cheered up when Carl visits. (Carl Larsson, painter of landscapes and domestic interiors.) Those apple cheeks, straw-yellow hair, eyes like hard blue sweets. When I tell him about my difficulties with the new crowd, he chuckles like a cartoon Santa.

—You no tempt them any more, sweetmeat? You no find some little hooks for to pull them out? Look, you can do like this, very easy . . .

With a bent pin, Carl coaxes a snail out of its shell and holds it up. For once the pungency of garlic outdoes the anise.

—You want?

—I don't eat any more.

—Ahhh. So you think you can do when we cannot?

—Muses are a special case. Anyway, I don't like snails.

—Some chocolate maybe?

Carl pulls a bag of broken chocolate from the pocket of his smock.

—Save it for a rainy day, Carl.

—*Ja, ja,* says Carl, momentarily pensive.

Carl really doesn't need my nagging when the sun is out. He's up with the lark, then, and out on the riverbank, throwing himself on his heaped palette like a ravenous man at a feast. Only in the rain when all the colour is drained from the landscape and the village becomes a daguerreotype of itself, he's restless and grumpy, clomping down the narrow corridor on thunderous clogs, slapping the walls with his broad, blunt hands. He knows that I can't control the climate. He knows too that there's plenty else for him to do indoors at the moment, like building a crib, for example. Carl is about to become a father, an event he's anticipating with glorious exuberance, but as yet he hasn't got around to much in the way of practical application. His wife Karin has almost reached term and Carl is still bellyaching about the rain. If only I could tell him that in time, rain and fatherhood will serve him well.

The candles have been blown out, the table cleared. Everyone has moved inside except Ramon who is attempting to plant a baguette in the middle of the garden. Dear oh dear, am I really here for this? Jan appears, carrying a neatly tied bag of rubbish to the wheelie bin in the courtyard. With this simple purpose in mind, he looks almost cheerful. On his return to the kitchen he stops politely to look at Ramon's bread plant. Jan would prefer to have wrapped up the baguette in cling film and put it in the fridge for breakfast but he smiles anyway.

While Ritta organises coffee and Calvados, Ramon wanders down to the river and communes with the drowned moon. Still sick from his last drinking binge and fighting the longing to join the others in a nightcap, the seconds stretch to eternity. In this he has my sympathy; for me too, time is always a tormentor. Edvard is ceremoniously laying a tray with little glasses, plain but pleasing cups and saucers, a plate of dark chocolate. A distant, private smile crinkles his tidy face as he carries the tray through to the sitting room which, for too long, has only been the meeting place of ghosts. Orange light spills into the courtyard as Ritta pours coffee and Edvard, enjoying his role of the perfect waiter, hands round Calvados.

I hear L's cough. (Louis, R.L.S., Stevenson, you'll know the name in some form.) It's deep tonight, like an axe splitting his ribs. Sometimes he changes his mind and doesn't call, just flits by the door and then I know things are bad. But tonight – I'm happy to say – he's visiting; pale, bright-eyed and shockingly slight. I pull out a chair for him, padding it with pillows from my bed. In spite of the sickness eating away at his body, L's mind is quicksilver. If the artists downstairs could see the dancing light in his eyes, his pitiful bird bones . . . And now he has met the American woman, he is a-flutter with love. Soon love and sickness will take him far from my not too comfortable armchair. I miss him already.

—You look well, I say, though he doesn't. He never does.

—I'm grand. On top of the world. This woman . . .

—I know.

—I can't describe the feeling, queenie, it's like something growing inside me, something sprouting and spreading . . .

L looks down at his lap and laughs.

—Don't I do that for you any more?

He laughs again, adjusts his muffler, shifts in his seat; he is never comfortable in one position for long.

—You know that without you, I'd be a nail lacking a hammer. But it's not quite the same . . .

I expect L to be too caught up with his own heart to be

interested in my problems with the artists but no, he wants to know all about them and listens intently to my reports on everyone's lack of progress, pulling thoughtfully on his inconsequential moustache.

—I don't envy you, queenie. A deil o a trauchle they're gien ye.

L begins coughing again, his chest snapping to his knees at each expectoration. He covers his mouth with a snowy handkerchief. It's not long now before he'll begin to spit blood. He pulls himself out of the chair and slips away. I can hear him coughing long after he leaves. I forgot to ask him about August's hallucinations.

From the window at the top of the stairs I can see the street. Already the Hotel de la Terrasse has closed its shutters though the same clutch of drinkers will still be inside. Directly above the boulangerie, the first-floor windows are wide open but the room is in darkness; I'm beginning to wonder whether L has been imagining things; his head is so full of stories that sometimes he confuses his internal life with the world outside. I lean on the window ledge, breathing in the anise-scented floor polish. The staircase is original. On the top step of the broad, deeply-scored oak boards a crude star has been gouged out – August? The flooring in the upstairs corridor is new, carefully stained to blend in with the staircase. At the join, woodworm has eaten away part of the step leaving a gash of darkness between old wood and new.

Ramon and Ritta are talking quietly in their room, Edvard is listening to Piaf regretting nothing for the third time this evening. From Jan's room, as always, no sound escapes. It's now several nights since the welcome dinner for Ritta and life has returned to its original state of strained solitude. Still, something may have come from the get-together. Ramon has stopped shaking. The morning after the welcome dinner, Jan threw himself into an aria about disintegration though by dinnertime it went in the wheelie bin along with the fag ends and the empties. Edvard has begun work on something which, he explained to me, represents a transitional state between need and desire. To my jaded eye, it looks like more coloured rings.

Above the boulangerie, lights are switched on and the small room leaps out into the darkness. Red and green spots beam inwards from the open window creating a suspended, open-air stage. A young voice begins to hum, there's some shuffling of feet and then he appears, just as L described him, a boy of eleven or twelve, stepping forward into the light, his serious eyes looking straight ahead into the darkness, silky black hair flashing red and green as he moves around behind the open window. One arm is buried up to the elbow in a red cotton devil complete with rubber horns and a long, coiling tail. On the other, a mermaid sways. The devil snakes towards the mermaid, the mermaid backs off, head bobbing, hair like bleached seaweed clinging to pearly breasts. As the devil moves into the green spot his grin turns luminous and lewd. The mermaid shimmies, blushes from head to fish tail. While he adjusts the lights, the boy drapes his puppets over the rusty, ornate railing. Still humming, his voice clear and sweet, he intensifies the red spot and removes a yellow filter, turning green back to blue. When he's satisfied with his alterations, he slips his hands back into the puppets and glances out into the darkness.

I wave. A mermaid and a devil wave back. The boy takes up a new position, hums another melody. He barely looks at what he's doing; it's not his eyes which guide him but some inner compass. The devil writhes in a red hell. The mermaid floats in a pool of celestial blue. For the first time in a long, long while I feel inspired.

The Four O'Clock Lady

ANITA DRAWS THE curtains, though there are only rooftops outside, pigeons and a couple of gargoyles. Frankie lets his head sink into the pillow and breathes in the smells of the room: lipstick, hot wax, nail polish, women. He tries not to look at the dreaded wall poster but, as always, he succumbs. It's like something from geography class at school, the earth sliced open like a layer cake, so that you could see how what goes on underneath the surface affects what happens on top. In this case it's a magnified cross-section of skin; pores like craters and thick, black hairs thrusting up from deep roots and covering the epidermal landscape with a horror forest of curving spikes.

Anita is her usual nice self, which is why Frankie always asks for her. It's bad enough coming week after week without having to suffer the blinking recoil of Karen, Pam, Angela. And Anita doesn't run late too often, which is another small relief. Waiting under the cruel lights of the salon foyer, which exaggerate every nick and bristle, is a humiliation he can do without. Waiting is hard enough without squirming on the dove-grey sofa under the disgusted scrutiny of the girls at the desk.

But the smaller salons were worse: poky, crummy little premises, where he had to hang about in full view of the street and worry about somebody he knew passing by and seeing him stuck there, waiting for a miracle. The treatments cost more in the department-store salon but the relative privacy was worth it. At least not just anybody might happen by and the clientele was mostly old dears who assumed, in an absent, self-absorbed way, that he was waiting for a girlfriend who was having her coiffure tidied up by Raphael or Rikki.

Frankie knows the names of most of the staff, at least those who stay and put up with the shitty pay and the snooty customers. Raphael's new and Rikki – who's been here for donkeys – is miffed that rather a lot of the ladies are asking for the new boy to tidy up their perms. Blue-black curls, chunky shoulders, a tan and a Venezuelan accent. And tight trousers, of course. Yes, Raphael is doing very nicely thank you with the ladies, cleaning up on tips and already picking up a few discreet requests for housecalls. Anita has told Frankie all about Raphael. Straight as a needle, unfortunately. It's only huffy, thinning-on-top Rikki who finds excuses to mince around the foyer, cologne floating in his wake like chiffon.

—Come as close as you can, says Anita.

The girls at the desk have a simple paging system: Pam, your three-thirty lady, Angela, your three-forty-five lady, and so on. The ladies, whose appointments haven't yet been announced over the tannoy, politely ignore Frankie, as they do each other. Like him, they come alone. They gaze at anti-wrinkle creams and bust-firming gels, or else rake voraciously through fashion mags. What do they feel when they're confronted by all those perfect teenage girls pouting at them, girls without a wrinkle, an ounce of fat, or an unwanted hair in sight? Why do they peer so intently at images of beauty and glamour which, with all the money in the world, are beyond them? Are they just looking for reminders of their youth, or is there something more predatory behind old birds devouring those flawless, teenage surfaces?

—Did your dentist friend give you something? says Anita.

—No.

Gold hoops their fingers, wrists, ears, throats; chains of the stuff but Frankie doesn't envy the ladies. Time, if not much else, is still on his side. Though by the end of the treatment, who knows? So slow, hair by hair, and how many will have to be burnt out at the root before he has any chance of becoming the divine creature he hopes will emerge from his superfluous forestation?

—That's a shame, says Anita.

—Mmmnnn, that little . . . arrangement fell through.

Such a slinky word, superfluous; it slides off the tongue like oil or honey. Realistically, it will probably take years to remove, patch by bristled patch. And the cost! If only Anita had something pretty on the wall, instead of that follicular nightmare.

—Oh dear, says Anita.

Anita doesn't wear jewellery. Just her white, short-sleeved overall, like a nurse's uniform. She even has an upside-down watch pinned to her breast pocket. Anita doesn't clink, like Karen or Pam or Angela, who flash cheap imitations of what their ladies wear against stringy old skin. Anita doesn't overdo the perfume or the make-up. The other girls wear foundation so thick you could scratch patterns on it, like tribal scars, make-up so thick their faces have become as blank and rubbery as mugger's masks. But hairless. Utterly hairless. Anita herself has just the faintest shadow of a moustache on her upper lip.

—I'll have to turn up the voltage, says Anita.
—OK.

Anita adjusts the overhead lamp and picks up her needle. Frankie's eyes close as he feels the needle come in contact with the dimple immediately beneath his lower lip. He hears the click as Anita switches on the power, and braces himself, wincing as the charge burns out one single follicle. So many more to go. Tears ooze though his squeezed-shut eyelids. But pain, Frankie knows, is relative.

—Sorry, says Anita.

The shots of novocaine had certainly helped, numbing Frankie's face long enough to endure a double treatment session without so much as a twitch. It had been a good enough arrangement at first, calling into Mervyn's surgery an hour before his appointment with Anita. Merv, with the mouthwash-blue eyes, antiseptic smile and surgical gloves, locking the door and cranking up the reclining chair so the two of them could exchange one good turn for another. But his dentist friend began stepping up his requests in a way which made thirty pain-filled minutes with Anita a safer option. Maybe in time he'd find another bent dentist for a trade-off but he's giving Merv the perv a wide berth. A chemist might be a better bet. One with a limited imagination.

Questions Frankie asks himself while Anita burns out hair follicles: *Why do you want to become a woman? Have you always wanted to be a woman? When did you first want to be a woman? Do you think your life will be better as a woman? Do you think a woman has a better life than a man? Do you realise that even with hormone injections, implants, surgery and years being Anita's four o'clock lady that you will still never be a real woman? Whose breasts will you have your implants modelled on, whose hips? Will the man of your dreams really want the manufactured woman-thing you'll become, or will you still, at the end of it all, be playing the same game without the equivalent bits?*

—Are you surviving? says Anita.
—Just about.

Anita will go on trying to help. That's her job. But she does more than her job. Anita, with her needle, in the tiny, curtained room high above the heart of the city, where every shelf is lined with creams promising epidermal miracles and the acned Anaglypta walls are blank apart from the awful poster. Anita provides a rest, a refuge.

—Those dizzies at the desk need specs. Four o'clock lady! I love it, really.

Once he's in Anita's warm, pink room, her little operating theatre, he's safe. Nothing she'll do, no matter how painful it might be at the time, will harm him. She knows and he knows that the treatment will take forever. She knows and he knows that, even with hormone treatment as well, the miracle might not happen. And even if it does, by the time it looks like taking, he might be past his sell-by date.

Anita is smiling and telling him about the suite she'd like; navy with orange pinstripes, from a place which specialises in Scandinavian design. She can't buy it yet, might never have enough spare cash, but it doesn't do any harm, she says, to keep a wee dream in your head. She knows and he knows that dreams are often better than the real thing.

—Sorry.

Anita says sorry a lot. Frankie knows that her sympathy is genuine. He knows, too, that it doesn't happen so often that you meet someone who means what they say. He knows about pretty promises, lovely lies he's wrapped around himself, nice nonsense said over showers, coffee, a line or two, get-up-and-go sounds. Thank yous and goodbyes, however they're phrased, the words like clothes are just a cover-up, but they get him up and out and home . . .

—Doing anything at the weekend? Anita asks.
—As much as possible.

Anita has a boyfriend. She is more or less living with him. They spend weekends in DIY shops, if you believe her. That is about as much as she'll say. Anita is really good at not talking about herself. And at not asking too many questions. Frankie imagines her on a Saturday night, out or more likely in with her nameless boyfriend – Frankie calls him Rock. A fire, a kitchen table, the flicker of the TV somewhere off to the side. A quiet, slightly boring Saturday night at home, she'll be in some kind of soft comfy jumper and Rock – he's probably called Colin or Sandy or Steve – will have his shirt open at the collar. They'll be sitting on the couch like an advert for cocoa, corny and cosy and just what Frankie would like for a change, a cosy, ordinary, safe night.

—What about you?
—Oh, nothing much, probably, says Anita.

You have to talk, though there isn't much time for talking. Only when Anita gives you a little break from the needle, which she always tries to do but her time is strictly limited. Anita's four-thirty lady has already been beamed across the tannoy, cutting in on a muted *Best of the Carpenters* cassette. Anita's next client is out in the foyer, early but nevertheless there, waiting on the sofa for her appointment, her miracle. The tannoy is an early warning that Frankie's time is almost up. Soon he'll be handing over his cash at the counter – including a generous tip for Anita – making his next appointment, nipping out the back door of the salon and down the stairs which lead directly to a side exit. In the early winter darkness, he'll slip, unnoticed, through the surf of shoppers and make his way, discreetly, to his next appointment.

Princess

—LOOK AT ME, look at me, look at me!

Sharon rolled into the room, arms outstretched and a huge grin on her face. Apart from the roller skates and a Disney tiara, she was wearing nothing at all. Robert picked up his camera and looked through the lens. His six-year-old daughter wobbled towards him, modelling the birthday presents he'd bought her and displaying, in her disregard for clothing, a delight which grabbed his heart and twisted it. He wanted a picture, a whole reel, wanted to preserve this moment as insurance against the future, a souvenir of this day together. He'd been needing something fresh and candid, he'd become too caught up in planned compositions, in thinking more than seeing. His students were learning to use their eyes first and their brain later while he'd been forgetting his own advice and thinking too much about the effects he wanted to achieve. He had lost his innocent attachment to the moment but here was his daughter, dazzling him with her smile and her happy absence of clothes, saying all there was to say about innocence.

He shut the lens and put down the camera.

—Go and put your clothes on, princess.

—I'm not cold, Dad. Why didn't you take any pictures of me?

—The film's finished, he lied. Put your clothes on and we'll go out to the park. Roller skates are really for outdoors.

—Aw Dad. You could send a picture to Mum to let her see what you gave me.

—Mum doesn't need one of my pictures. She can see the roller skates whenever she wants. You'll be taking them . . . *home* . . . with you.

It burnt his mouth to say the word and mean a place where he didn't live any more.

—But I want you to take some pictures.

—We'll buy a film when we go out. I could take some pictures in the park.

—Call me princess again. I like it when you call me princess.

—We could stop at the ice-cream shop, too. Get you a double scoop seeing as it's your birthday. OK?

—OK, Dad.

Lies and bribery. The kind of things Robert didn't want his daughter to encounter but here he was, resorting to them himself. But he couldn't explain to her, he wouldn't tell the stupid truth about why he stopped himself taking any pictures. She wouldn't understand, couldn't. She had not yet been corrupted by the adult world – at least he hoped this much was true – and corruption can only be understood by those who've had acquaintance with it.

As Sharon rumbled down the hall, Robert closed his eyes and imagined the photo of his daughter that he couldn't take. It would have to be a memory, her pink translucent skin, her chubby knees, rounded tummy . . . even in his mind he was censoring himself, avoiding certain body parts, picturing her without sexual characteristics, the way dolls used to be made, though nowadays many came complete with anatomically accurate genitals. But even this neutered, censored image felt questionable now. With the custody battle turning sourer by the day, could every gesture of affection between himself and his daughter now come under scrutiny, every touch be open to misinterpretation, to distortion?

—Dad, Dad . . . can you help me?

Sharon was wearing a dress which buttoned down the back, but no underwear. He did up the buttons and awkwardly tied the bow at her waist.

—Go and find some pants, Sharon.

—Nobody's going to see my bum under a dress are they?

—Put some on anyway. You'll catch a chill.

—Daaaad! It's hot. I'm sweating.

—Put some pants on or we're not going for ice cream.

Sharon's lip wobbled.

—It's my birthday, she wailed. Why are you being so horrible?

—Please, Sharon. Just do it and then we'll go out. We'll have a nice time. I've been looking forward to seeing you so much.

—Will you do my hair in plaits, then, like Mum does?

—I'm no good at that, princess. I'll make a mess of it. That was true enough. But he'd learn.

—I like your flat, Daddy.

—That's good. You can come whenever you want.

—Can I? Can I really? Yeaaaahhh!

Sharon's explosions of enthusiasm startled him these days. He'd expected the break-up to sully her, to turn an exuberant child into a glum, taciturn one but it hadn't happened. Not yet, at any rate. She was still brim-full of life and he loved her more than ever for it. There had been tears of course, plenty, of sadness, incomprehension, rage but in between the tears, her eyes were still radiant.

—You'll have to ask Mum, of course. But I don't mind how often you come or how long you stay. Remember that, Sharon. My flat is your home too.

—Why would Mum mind?

—I don't know. She might have other plans. Some days it might be difficult for her to bring you over.

—If I put on some pants, will you try and do my hair in plaits?

Robert's attempts at fixing Sharon's hair turned into the disaster he'd expected it to be. Sharon screeched and yowled as he tried to brush out tangles and was disgusted by her father's loose, lumpy plaits. After several attempts to improve them he lost his patience and told her she'd have to learn to do her hair by herself or choose something easier. In the naked scorn blazing from her eyes, he saw the best and the worst of her mother: Avril's invincible will, a will which had carried them all through hard times together and now, he was sure, would keep her going without him.

The park was mobbed. He'd forgotten to bring his camera but it was probably just as well. As he held Sharon's arm to steady her as she skated, Robert kept a look out for stones, glass, dogs, cyclists; dangers. Now he worried more about her than when they'd been all together as a family, now it was vital that he return Sharon to Avril exactly as she'd arrived; even a grazed knee or the beginnings of a cold could suggest lack of attention, of care. No, his daughter must be returned to her mother in perfect condition, like a gift.

Sharon tugged at Robert's arms.

—Look Dad, look Dad.

A ring of ragged youngsters sprawled on the grass, drinking wine, playing guitars and decorating each other's hair with beads and rows of tiny plaits.

—Janie's got a wee plait just like that in her hair, it's got five blue beads in it, Dad. She got it done at the craft market. D'you think that lady would do one for me, if I asked? We could give her money. Janie said it cost two pounds something. Will you ask, Dad, please? If you haven't enough money I could pay you back. I've got seven pounds sixty-seven pence. Please, Dad.

—You can't just go up to somebody and ask them to do your hair. And it would take ages . . .

—Will you give me a piggy-back then? I'm tired.

—You're getting a bit big for piggy-backs. And heavy with those skates on.

—I've been skating for ages, Dad. Why won't you do anything I want?

Robert sat down on a bench and eased her on to his back. He should have been more organised and got out of town for the afternoon even if Avril had shown up two hours later than agreed. The grime of the city and the smell of picnics hung over the park. By the time everyone went away that night, the grass would be barely visible beneath the rubbish people left behind them. It was always the same after a good day. He should know. Sleeping at night had become impossible. Night after night he'd lain awake, listening to unfamiliar noises in the flat: creaks, groans, clicks and drips and an unsettling powdery sound in the wall behind his bed, like crumbling masonry. He imagined the tenement disintegrating little by little so that nobody noticed until it was too late to stop the erosion, too late to do anything other than stare open-mouthed at a pile of debris, the remains of homes, lives. At night, too, it was always harsh, pain-laden human sounds which carried the most: drunks roaring at real or imaginary assailants, bawling babies, couples fighting outside or in. When he heard a couple going for each other he found himself listening intently, greedily almost, trying to picture their faces, the inside of their flats, their beds, trying to work out what had turned lovers into enemies.

He'd been lying awake at night, getting up at dawn and going to the park with his camera to catch the gulls doing their dawn raids on the rubbish left on the grass. There was something intimidating about the big birds striding around in the first light, clean, cruel and faintly amused, like thugs or generals. On the third morning he'd almost got himself arrested. Crouched down behind a tree he'd been waiting for them to land on the grass when a young woman jogger had rounded the bend in the circuit. At the same moment he'd sprung forward, aiming his lens at the gulls. The woman screamed and broke into a sprint, blowing a whistle as she ran. Knowing how quickly the birds would leave again, he continued taking photographs. A park patrol van drew up beside him. The dour, putty-faced warden wasn't at all convinced by his interest in gulls and rubbish; apparently the jogger had claimed that Robert had been photographing her.

—As you'll no doubt have noticed, sir, the young lady was wearing brief, shiny shorts.

Robert laughed out loud. He hadn't noticed the jogger's clothing; he'd been too jarred by her fear to notice anything much. Besides, he was trying to photograph the gulls and rubbish. Brief, shiny shorts, Christ. The warden had certainly been paying close attention.

—If I find you and your camera here again at this time of the morning, sir, you'll be paying a visit to the station.

Sharon's skates banged against his ribs as he lumbered past a cricket game, a football game, a picnicking family: father, mother, a granny, a couple of toddlers trying to turn cartwheels on the grass, and a baby crashed out in a pushchair, its cheeks like tomato skins. Granny was reading the newspaper, the mother peeling boiled eggs, the father pouring juice into coloured plastic beakers. Sharon dragged heavily on his shoulders.

—I wish I had a brother or sister. Look at the baby, Dad. It's so cute!

—It's got sunburn. It should be taken home.

Home home home.

—Choose, Sharon. Two scoops and then we can get going, OK?

Sharon, mesmerised by the tubs of ice cream, had her face pressed against the glass counter; lemon, pistachio, caramel, chocolate, mint, tangerine and some violent pink stuff, gleamed frostily. A queue was gathering behind them.

They made their way home even more awkwardly than before, Sharon trying to lick her scoops of chocolate and tangerine alternately, Robert clutching her arm. Roller skates and ice cream at the same time, he realised too late, were not a good idea. In the heat the ice cream was melting quickly and he'd forgotten to bring any tissues with him. He seemed to be having to learn things all over again, things he thought he already knew.

—Try and lick the drips, Sharon, he said but it wasn't easy for the child to turn the cone round with one hand. She lost her balance and lurched off to the side.

—Careful!

—I can't help it, Dad!

Her hands and face were already smeared with ice cream and it was only a matter of time until some brown or orange sludge would find its way on to her dress – a birthday present from Avril – buttercup-yellow and white, flimsy stuff which would stain in a minute. He knew enough about laundry problems. Working from home, he'd done most of the laundry. He had plenty experience of ruined children's clothes – food, paint, glue, grass, mud, blood, vomit, all contributed indelible stains. It had occurred to him once or twice while he was sorting out the whites from the coloureds that there was maybe some kind of record in stained clothing, some kind of statement about the world he lived in, that it might have been worth trying a series of photos before he threw the clothes into the washing machine, but he'd never got around to it. Now he used the launderette once a week; yes, some things were easier.

Sharon's ice cream was barely half-eaten when it fell out of its cone, slithered down her dress and plopped on to the pavement. An empty soggy cone, the dress a God-awful mess. Tears and more tears. Roller skates and ice cream, why was he so stupid? Sharon wanted to go back for another but Robert knew he had to get the dress in water as soon as possible.

—Next time you come over we'll go without the roller skates. We could sit in and order one of the fancy sundaes.

—With a sparkler in it?

—Whatever you want, princess.

Robert washed out Sharon's dress, scrubbing and scrubbing at the sticky stains, holding the cloth up to the light every so often, going at the marks again and again.

Laying out the birthday tea, it already felt like a long day. Sharon had unwillingly agreed to put on the dress meant for the next day, her going-home dress. He should have tried to invite some of her friends round, done something more to celebrate the occasion. He'd been lucky enough to have his daughter over for her birthday and – selfishly perhaps – didn't want to share her with anyone. Though a party would have been more cheerful for the child than his own tense company, the break-up had been so recent and bitter he couldn't contemplate other parents arriving in his thrown-together shoebox of a flat, looking around, checking the place out, checking him out. *Could he cope, was he safe to leave their precious children with?* He wasn't ready for that kind of scrutiny, not now, not yet. Next year, maybe. Maybe by this time next year he and Avril would be able to stand in the same room together, smiling and offering round trays of sandwiches and cakes.

—Mum says I've to have a bath if you've got any clean towels.

—Of course I've got clean towels. What's she talking about?

—I don't know, Dad. She just said it and I'm just telling you because it's what she said. Can I have a party next year and you and Mum both come?

—We'll see.

—That's what grown-ups say when they mean no.

—It's too far away to think about.

They had played draughts and pick-up sticks, built several castles from bricks and painted a picture together. Sharon had splashed around in the bath, the wet dress hanging on the pulley above her and dripping coldly on to her hair. Then they'd watched too many cartoons. Sharon hadn't wanted to go to bed and Robert had let her stay up much later than Avril had suggested – as if he didn't know her bedtime – so late that she fell asleep on the couch, thumb in her mouth, a habit she'd given up before she learned to walk. He carried her, heavy with sleep, through to the flimsy camp-bed in the study. She seemed to have grown since he last saw her, only a week ago. Soon he'd need to get her a better bed and turn his darkroom into a proper bedroom. Or give her his room and get a fold-out couch for the living room. Whatever.

Robert was woken in the night by Sharon running down the hall and into his room.

—Had a bad dream, Mummy.

—Dad, Sharon, it's Dad here.

—Had a bad dream, Dad.

She climbed into the bed beside him and lay rigid, staring up into the darkness. He reached out and held her hand while she calmed down.

—I'll take you back to bed now, come on. The bad dream's finished now.

—I want to sleep in your bed.

—I don't think so.

—Mummy lets me sleep in her bed.

—Please, Sharon, it's late. Let me take you through. I'll stay with you for a bit.

—NO, NO, NO!

Robert lay beside his daughter, stroking her cheek, lifting a lock of hair away from her eyes, inhaling her warm breath, humming a tune he'd sung to her as a baby, hearing his voice trembling, hearing it crack like a reed, a thin, lost sound, his own voice in the dark.

Static

THERE'S SOMETHING I'D like to experience before I die. In some parts of the world, prairie, pampas, steppe, veldt – a wide open space where thunderclouds roll across the sky and dust balls roll across the ground – it happens. But maybe the place doesn't really matter, maybe it could happen anywhere and it would prove the thing scientifically, it would make sense of the invisible workings of bodies and minds. At some time or other we've all felt the jolt and maybe we spend the rest of our lives trying to recapture that vital shock. You will know what I mean. We may have different ways of describing the sensation but both of us believe that it can be found, if the conditions are met.

One condition, an essential one, is not to try too hard, so I haven't gone to too much trouble, just a little trouble, in case you might think I hadn't made any effort at all. I'm wearing something nice but not too nice, not my favourite clothes; that would be taking too much of a risk. Going through my wardrobe, I tried to imagine how you might react to the colour of a dress, the fabric of a skirt, the cut of a pair of jeans, discovering that my wardrobe doesn't contain many articles of clothing that I like. Though I did buy for myself more or less everything I own, the choice, in the end, was limited.

I hope, too, that you'll wear something I like a little but not too much. I don't want to feel intimidated by your clothes. Or your appearance. Your appearance does matter – not so much what you've inherited but what you've done with yourself since. It's better you look quite nice but not perfect. Your voice, too, matters, your smell, the texture of your skin. Though I'm very far from perfect you might like some things about me. My teeth are reasonable and, as they are, I smile a lot, which makes me appear to be a cheerier person than I really am. I had my hair trimmed a couple of weeks ago so it's tidier than usual and I've found a rinse which replaces the grey with gold. Instead of dreary wintry tones, I now have summery glints through my otherwise unexceptional brown hair. With the help of some inexpensive tubes of ammonia-free colour, I intend to go slowly blonde.

The flat – I've cleaned and tidied and spruced it up a bit but mostly because I prefer it that way; a clean house feels happier than a dirty one. I've watered the plants and sprayed their leaves so they glisten like freshly showered skin. Would you prefer my fleshy succulents or the feathery scented geraniums? Do you know that geraniums are named after crane bills? If so, do you find this fact as comical as I do? I considered buying flowers to put about the place but buying flowers for myself always feels dismal or extravagant and neither mood is appropriate. Of course I changed the sheets and aired the bedroom. No stale odours or memories cling to my dusted walls.

Of course you may not see my home. You may see nothing of my hand-sewn curtains, my scrubbed skirting boards, my pressed linen and polished woodwork, or the tidy pile of ongoing projects which keep me busy and hopeful most of the time. You may not see any of it but if you do, I'd like it to be in reasonable order, I'd like my home to be wearing its welcoming, capable face.

If you are in my home you should be able to look around it and discover something – but not too much – of me. Rather a lot of me, possibly too much, has been put into paintwork and curtains and carefully considered linen but you have to put yourself somewhere, don't you? Some people leave themselves around all over the place but not me. I wonder whether you ever feel you have put too much of yourself into what could manage quite well without your efforts. Have you, too, come to the conclusion that all the bits and bobs around you will go on existing perfectly well without you taking any notice whatsoever? Do you, in greyer moods, feel this can also be true of people?

There is food, in case it's required, though sometimes food is just an added complication; accompanied consumption isn't always a plain, shared pleasure. Too much attention can be paid to the wrong details. Think, for example, about the crockery and ovenware, the clinking and pinging, the faffing around with ladles and asbestos gloves. Putting a meal on the table involves contact with so many inert, cumbersome objects when they are not the point at all. And the eating itself, the chomping and chewing and swallowing, the forkfuls of food to be negotiated from plate to mouth; perhaps we should rule out eating but just in case food turns out to be an essential condition, I set the table, remembering to check the cutlery for streaks.

The food itself; if you didn't like my cooking, would it be something we could ignore or would it lessen the voltage ever so slightly? Would we find ourselves shifting in our seats and turning our eyes and thoughts to something other than each other? If there is food, perhaps it should have nothing whatsoever to do with me or you, food which someone, somewhere else has made, food which has been purchased from a pretty boy or girl in a smart shop, though that too might be dampening, the lack of interest, effort. Even if the food is too wonderful and exotic for me to have attempted to make, offering you a precooked meal seems a bit like a trick, like cheating and cheating is not attractive unless it is clever and dramatic, the way it's portrayed in films and plays. In life it's small, mean and grubby.

The weather is good and it might be better to be outdoors although – as you'll have noticed – as soon as the sun shines, the world is crammed with courting couples and families milling around whatever green space they can find. All these other attached people might be a bit distracting. And the public setting might feel a bit obvious, contrived; strolling among so many composite blocks of humanity, maintaining a suitable, single distance . . . maybe not.

Thinking can get in the way, can't it, so once I've sorted out my thoughts enough but not too much, I'll slip you to the back of my mind, pop you into my mental glory-hole. If you could look inside, you'd see my most cherished moments all piled in together, squirrelled away, comforters to bring out on cold, dark days when I can't see beyond my own blanket of boredom. Don't worry, I'm very greedy when it comes to cherished moments; I'll share them with nobody, not even you.

To think that such an amazing thing can happen in what can't, by the sounds of it, be a very interesting place. Prairie, pampas, steppe, veldt. A whole lot of nothing much. A landscape of absence. But maybe absence meets the conditions, maybe a certain level of lack is required.

Friends, some of whom are familiar with the not-so-cherished moments of my life, have not been informed. (You, I promise, won't hear about those mostly minor calamities; there will be no sob stories, no confessions, above all not even the slightest hint of desperation because that would set up a different kind of circuit; one of sympathy, need.) I have managed to avoid any mention of you. Friends, I know too well, would gulp down all the details that I was willing to provide – as if they were olives, peanuts, popcorn – concerning your looks, personality, politics, bank balance and, of course, marital status. Married or divorced are, now, the most likely options. And then there would be the inevitable if tacit speculation on other intimate details. Friends would shuffle the facts and build up their own fancy-enhanced images of you, which I'm sure would be nothing at all like mine. They'd pass judgement. I don't mean to be hard on my friends – I love them dearly most of the time – but I've learned from past mistakes that it's not always beneficial to listen to advice. I can go into a day feeling briefly, recklessly *engaged* in it, until some good advice is poured into my ear and blights my little bud of hope.

So I have been keeping you a secret. There have been times when I've been tempted to slip a *By the way* into the many and interminable conversations about other people's husbands, wives, lovers, children, which I find myself dragged into, like a recalcitrant mule. There have been times when I've had the desire to mention ever so casually that, even in the emotional desert – which, it's assumed, my industrious, single life has been for a little too long – between you and me, if the conditions are met, a literal, visible charge just might – as can happen in other, similarly monotonous landscapes – crackle and leap across the void.

After the Gun

He put the gun in his mouth. It was cold but he held it in his mouth until it reached body heat. He felt calm, sure that, for once, he was doing the right thing when he released the catch and squeezed the trigger.

It is raining hard. He backs off into the shop doorway, a crumpled, cod-eyed slither shrinking from his own reflection in the glass, hand flying to his face. The limp, the stoop are self-induced, brought on by habitual shielding of one side of his face. It had to be hidden, had to be, not because it was disfiguring – which it was, hugely, a slack pouch of skin hanging from his jaw like a goitre – but because when people saw it, they knew. It was the pity he shrank from, the patronising pity of strangers.

She knows. He knows the look; the eyes flaring, mouth muscles snapping. Her dark eyebrows dip, knit together briefly as she fixes her expression, makes it as neutral as she can. It's not easy for her. The young woman has a restless, open face but doesn't want her shock to show. He backs off against the wet window and hides his face behind his hand.

Since his mistake of staying alive, he feels very small, though he is a tall man who looks older than his years because of the stoop. His need to shrink, to retract from the glance of strangers, ages him. It is not so bad, though. He is not so bad. There are others much worse; he only has to look up from those drab gutters he searches so intently when people pass. Much of his retrieved life is spent affecting interest in cracked flagstones, fag ends, dog turds, shrugging the collar of his raincoat up over his cheek. But it is not the appearance in itself; it is the sign, the significance. He is known by this, by this sign of a God-awful cock-up. It is humiliating beyond words.

—I like the rain, she says.

—So do I, so do I.

His words slur. He sounds drunk, which he is not in the least.

—But I like the sun better.

—Yes, so do I.

—All this wet and dark, it can bring you down, can't it?

—Yes, yes it can.

He is trying very hard to make his words clear, to force them through his numb lopsided mouth in such a way that they come out even, balanced. He does not want this woman's pity. Nor her fear. What he wants is something altogether different. He wants . . . But her eyes slip away, they have seen the sale shoes in the window behind him and she's concentrating on them, deliberately. She does not have to feel guilty about this, about considering some possible purchase for herself. It wasn't as if he were poor, no, that was something else everybody knew; rich enough to loaf his life away and so, in the places he frequented, the dark, anonymous places he was drawn to, pity was almost always spiked with contempt. But when was it ever pure, when was pity ever more than a twisted insult?

Her eyes slip away from his dogged, resurrected face – reincarnation could never be on his cards, only this monstrous resurrection – the face that was meant to have been blown off, erased but instead looms out from shadows to jolt the unsuspecting into whispering: *What's he like, the man who tried to kill himself?*

And failed. Missed. At such close range the odds against missing must have been sky-high. Of all the possibilities open to him – and there are a surprising number of suicide options – the gun had seemed to be the most reliable. Almost impossible to fail but he'd done so, on a monumental scale, and it is the sign of his monumental failure which makes people catch their breath and turn away. He does not want to frighten anybody, the whole point was to do away with fear, annihilate it, in himself, the family, the ever-decreasing clutch of friends, the whole point was to remove the source, the cause. And now the family are ever more fearful, for him, for themselves. And ashamed. And it's hard to tell which, for them, is worse. They can afford many things but not shame, no more shame.

—I think if we got a bit of sun here on a regular basis, we'd have a whole different country. A bit of sun lifts the spirit, don't you think?

—I expect so.

—Do you always agree with people, or just with strangers?

—Usually I don't talk to strangers.

This is a lie. He talks to strangers if he talks to anyone.

—Usually strangers don't talk to me.

This is more accurate.

The woman has stopped looking at shoes, has turned her back on them. Like him, she leans against the glass and stares at the street, where the rain rattles off the cobbles like birdshot. Office workers slant past, wrapped up in raincoats and thoughts of home. He's been walking in the rain for too long, as usual, but can't yet face the comforts of home. Some days, most days, are like this. Last night, again, he behaved badly. Difficult not to, when the family watched over him with sly, devoted vigilance, as if, God forbid, he might try it again.

It had been raining that day, pissing down on the roof of the garden shed in an endless plash. Fittingly dreich, fittingly relentless for what he'd planned. It had been taking shape in his mind for long enough, for ever it felt like, as if his whole life had been a preparation for that moment. He'd felt a brief churn of pride, of heroism even, an inner glow where, for so long, nothing had managed to flush out the chill.

He'd cleared a space on the rickety trestle table which held Edwina's seed trays and wobbly stacks of flowerpots. For years Edwina had lavished attention on her sun-loving tomatoes and every year she was disappointed; the harvest never amounted to more than a handful of shrunken, misshapen fruits, which no one could bring themselves to eat. The frail fronds had quivered as he pushed seed trays to the side, blew crumbs of compost off the table's coarse surface and took out pen and paper.

He'd wanted to put it down properly, wanted to get the words right because he'd got them so wrong up till now. There must be no smell of drink on the words, nothing to suggest that his action was in any way impulsive and, for once, he'd felt totally in control; his hand hadn't shaken when he'd written: My dearest ones . . . his hand hadn't shaken and it hadn't been so terribly difficult, explaining, while Edwina and the boys were elsewhere, unconcerned.

* * *

It is the concern, the persistent, reproachful concern that has become so difficult, the monitoring of his every sigh and silence, the obligation to behave properly. Before the gun, the family had let him be; Edwina, bless her, had always been a devotee of making the best of things. But after the gun, after his face was grafted back on as best it could be – which was, to be honest, bloody awful – after he was well and truly back in the land of the living, the family's bitter vigilance took root.

—It's the world we live in, says the woman. We're too suspicious to talk to strangers. Sad really.

—Yes . . . yes.

—There you go again, agreeing with me.

She is too close. He can see faint creases on her cheeks and a mesh of tiny lines around her eyes; laughter lines, but she isn't laughing; she's staring boldly, rudely even, at his eyesore of a face. It is all he can do not to turn on his heels and splash off into the rain.

—Is it a barny you're after?

—Well, it's not much of a conversation if you keep saying *yes* all the time.

—Do you want a conversation?

—It would pass the time while we wait for the rain to go off.

—Will it go off?

—Soon. Those folk on the street should have stayed where they were a bit longer.

—Maybe they like the rain.

—Nobody likes getting soaked.

—Maybe they've no choice.

—There's always a choice.

—No, no there isn't.

—That's better. You disagreed with me. Go on then. Don't stop when you're just getting started.

The woman, hands on hips, grins and turns up her sharp little chin. He leans forward, bending towards her so that his muzzled words might be decipherable above the din of the rain. He is too close.

—Can I ask you a question?

—I don't think so.

—You don't have to answer. But you can't really stop me asking, can you?

Oh yes he could. He could stalk away from her without saying another word, without ever speaking to her again. He could leave her there, waiting confidently for the rain to go off, and go home. Or else to the casino, the bars, the cinema. He likes the cinema, its warm sweaty darkness in which he can, on occasion, feel part of something intimate and invisible.

When he'd finished the letter – how long those few words had taken to write – he stood up. With his back pressed against the window, blotting out the sludgy green light, he raised the gun, slid it down the length of his tongue and it was only then that his hand shook, that he made the error which was to cost him his death.

—So what do you want to know? he says.

—Oh, you know.

—Do I?

—You're being really difficult.

—Isn't that what you want?

His mouth twists into a hideous approximation of a smile.

—You want to know about this?

—I'm just making conversation. The rain will be off soon. It's going to be a fine evening.

The sky is beginning to clear, lighten, to stretch out thin and filmy above the rooftops which descend like steps to the hazy, blue-grey firth. That day, when he'd locked himself in the shed with Edwina's tomato plants, writing paper and the gun, he'd felt unaccountably happy, the way he does now. But it's different now. He's different now.

Consider Yourself Kissed

THE BLUE HYDRANGEA heads are dotted around the tables: squat, chubby blossoms in their little cellophane skirts; scentless and showy, not my type of flower at all. Too sturdy, regular, too sure of itself. Bougainvillea I like; the delicate, flimsy blooms have a depth, a passion to them. There is no depth to hydrangea. They are a flat, waxy reliable blue, like railing paint.

I can't talk about flowers to Gleason though I can talk about railings. Gleason has been putting up railings everywhere, even on the balcony, making our new apartment secure. I tell him crown-of-thorns works better than any railing for keeping thieves at bay but Gleason believes man's inventions are superior to nature. Besides, he likes a job to be done and that's it, finished. No upkeep. No maintenance. Clean-cut. Something definite, final and railings don't need cutting back like crown-of-thorns.

But these new railings we have need paint. I can't live my life behind black bars, even if they're special fancy ironwork with loops and curlicues. Black railings are never pretty, I tell Gleason and what is life worth if your home is a prison? He says,

—If you don't like the black, I'll paint them blue, so when you stand on the tiled balcony and look out, all you'll notice is the sky.

Gleason believes in working from the inside out, so while he was taking care of the bedroom bolts and bars on the bathroom window – which is too small for even a child thief to squeeze through – I decided to try some crown-of-thorns at street level. Not even the craziest house-breaker would try to cross my hedge; beneath the red bracts lurks a more vicious deterrent than barbed wire. The problem now is keeping the hedge under control; it has grown, like everything does here, fast and furious, sprawling over the pathway. Tonight, on the way out, I gashed my knee on my own protection system. Blood spattered my dancing shoes. I was lucky not to ruin my new dress.

All the way along the street I could hear the music and the cars pulling up and skidding on the dry earth around the gymnasium. The air is so sweet tonight, intoxicating, like the memory of a caress. Night scents are always the sweetest, though often they're produced by plain plants. I would have liked to take my time, to enjoy the coolness, inhale slowly and deeply, savour the air but I was late. A sharp little pain burned in my chest as I hurried along. The dance must already be in full swing and all too soon it would be over.

I am very happy with Gleason but there are times when I feel . . . shut in. Tonight, as I sped along the seams of the dress which I was rushing like mad to finish, because nothing fits since the last time I went dancing, he hovered on the balcony. He hovered and fussed with his elaborate system of locks and bolts. Sometimes the extra security makes me feel insecure. Put up a fence, you invite a stranger to break it down. Think about something all the time, it's going to happen.

—Go ahead without me, I say. I'll join you soon. Consider yourself kissed.

His fussing distracted me, slowed me down and made me cross.

I don't want to be cross with Gleason. He is thinking only of the best for us and I know something has to be done. There have been nights when I too have lain awake, unable to identify a sound among the frogs hammering on the pond, the cicadas drilling holes in the darkness, banana palms snapping under the weight of their fruit – there are a score of sounds I could name – nights when I was convinced I could hear papery whispers and the dull pad of bare feet, nights when I lay still as a lizard, barely breathing.

But mostly, knowing that Gleason is there in the bed beside me, I can give myself up to the luxury of sleep, assured that nothing can disturb us, nothing leap out of the darkness. And even if it did, it wouldn't get through Gleason's lines of defence; no, I am well protected.

How pretty the students look in their perky white suits, berets perched on their heads. Gleason is supervisor to twenty student teachers, girls with little ambition other than to find a husband, soon. When you're paid less than a cleaner you don't see teaching as a long-term vocation. Their energy and enthusiasm will be sapped from them slowly but surely: no, cleaning is a more rewarding occupation. You see results, make people happy, in a small way. A teacher encounters too much failure. I know.

When I met Seph – and married him almost immediately – I was a tired-out teacher. Not that marriage improved my own circumstances in any practical way. *Husband* is not a correct description of what Seph was to me. People say love is about chemistry, well, Seph and I had the kind of chemistry which mostly made explosions. By ourselves we might have been two stable substances but together – blue flashes and a smell of burning.

So many people are up dancing that there are plenty empty tables near the floor. I sit at one and wait for Gleason to finish his social duties and find me. He is congratulating his students for passing their exams and wishing them luck for the future. In his professional role, he is so relaxed, so expansive, a man at ease with the world, and himself. I note the girls who kiss him twice and those who kiss him three times as he takes his leave from them, leisurely, so leisurely, to join his new wife. I pay particular attention to the three-kiss girls; two of them. For one it's a stagy affectation, a habit picked up from the television. The other I'm not so sure. Less flourish. More intensity. Is it a hint that she's available or is she just following a trashy fashion? The three-kiss habit is tricky. It's the accompanying gestures, the flutter of an eyebrow, the clasp of hands, list of the body that you have to pay attention to. With the second three-kiss girl, Gleason's embrace is distinctly more than a grazing of cheeks. I crinkle the hydrangea's cellophane skirt. Do I care about this?

The waiter comes over to my table and sweeps the empty plastic beer cups on to the concrete floor. This is the worst thing about the new building regulations – how can anyone dance on concrete? A dead floor; still, even over concrete it is possible, with the right partner, to feel weightless . . .

The fashion is shorts and miniskirts again this year, nothing with a swing to it, nothing which gives itself to the music. But I like watching the dancers, the showy and the shy, the graceful and oddly awkward, complete strangers, couples who have been too close for too long, those lit up by love or dulled by disappointment. I know most of the people here. When you're the only hairdresser in town, you get to know a lot of people. In a small way, of course. And they know me. In a small way.

Gleason has worked through the sailor-suited girls to my table. He's got a swagger on him as he says, in his old-fashioned but lovable way:

—Here I am, dear, to take care of you.

Anywhere other than a dance floor and I'd be more than happy but not here, not now. The dance floor is not at all the place for Gleason to take care of me. Though I didn't come here just to spectate, though I'm itching to move with the music, my foot stops tapping, my bones set into a rigid wall against the beat.

If somebody would just come and join us, interrupt us, detain us at the table, let us be the happy new couple that we are. But his students have turned back to their boyfriends, Gleason is standing over me, offering his arm, his secure, protective arm. I smooth down my dress and let him lead me on to the floor.

Gleason presses his cheek against mine. His breath is hot and enthusiastic. He is a noisy breather, even when he is not exerting himself. That and the teeth sucking I don't like. Nor the way he rolls up his vest when it's hot, to air his belly. I don't mind his bigness, I'm no string bean myself, but why draw attention to your fondness for beer? But these are silly things and tonight Gleason's not slobbing around in a vest, no, he's spruced up, smart, in black trousers and blue dress shirt. I should be, *would* be proud of him, anywhere but on the dance floor.

Gleason whirls me round the room, fast, too fast, racing the beat, unable to hear the way it pulls back, hesitates, changes direction, tone, missing all the small twists and turns which make the tune beautiful, seductive. It's disappointing in a man so particular about the details when it comes to railings and pathways. But music, to Gleason, is only a pattern of notes. As he is counting out five, six, seven, eight into my ear, Seph and his new girlfriend brush past us and I lose the rhythm entirely.

Seph: I don't want Seph and he doesn't want me. We both knew this, felt it long before we were able to put it into words, before were able, finally, to part. And now we have our separate, better lives. Gleason and I have our differences but they are easy differences – like about the railings – they can be smoothed out or covered up and ignored. Gleason and I do not share big, painful differences, which is why we have such a secure arrangement, why we are a good partnership.

—Maybe we should sit down, I say, after the third dance in a row. My dress is crushed to a rag where his hands have been, in spite of the good fabric. Seph's hands never left a mark on my dresses.

—But you love dancing.

—Let's get a beer.

—But you don't like beer. And they're playing samba. You love samba.

—I'm thirsty, Gleason.

—Didn't you have wine earlier?

I call the waiter, order beer and sit down. Gleason sits down too, after wiping some crumbs off his seat. He is about to lecture me on the dangers of mixing grape and grain when he sees the gash on my leg. It looks quite dramatic when the flashing stage lights hit it, a dark zigzag.

—Whatever happened?

It's nothing, but it gives me an excuse to sit out the samba. I explain about the crown-of-thorns and straight away Gleason's fear of calamity overwhelms him.

There's something toxic in the thorns, he tells me, highly toxic. To be on the safe side, I should really have a tetanus injection, though it's an hour's drive to the hospital, a long wait is inevitable, it's very late already, and maybe, all things considered, it might be better to go home and dab on some arnica – Gleason believes this plant cures everything from backache to warts – and review the situation in the morning. One thing is certain, the crown-of-thorns will have to go. First thing in the morning. If it can't be dug up, it'll be burnt. After the recent drought, it will go up like a torch. But if the crown-of-thorns is removed, there will be inadequate security and didn't I see now that it would have been more sensible to fence in the whole place straight away?

The band is preparing for its final session; a keyboard is exchanged for an accordion, tambourines and maracas are raised high, the singer adjusts his velvet bow tie, the guitarist drags a handkerchief across his face. The baby-faced band sticks with popular dance tunes in spite of disco effects; blue smoke billowing up from the back of the stage and a tiresome sequence of flashing lights. Waiters hurry to and fro with last orders of beer and fried potatoes. The debris is swept up, the potted hydrangea heads plucked from the tables and set in serried ranks along the front of the stage like a little blue platoon.

At the far side of the floor you're standing, watching the dancers. It's a happy night, isn't it, Seph? Some of the students have been celebrating a bit too much – and why not – and the queues for the toilets are spilling into the main hall and, of course, when that happens the boys just step outside and relieve themselves in among the cars and courting couples, as the big, stunned moths whirr around the streetlights.

We wouldn't have been found outside a dance hall, would we, pressed against a wall, not, at least, until the band had packed up their instruments, the lights had been turned off and the moths had fluttered back into the dark. When music was playing, we spent every moment on the floor. It was only later, at home, that it was difficult being close, only later that we slid apart; clumsy, tense, and the right words would never come to make those bad times better.

I'd curl up in a sheet, bury my face in the pillow, pretend to sleep because it was better than fighting. You would go out on the balcony and drink, or roam the streets all night.

You don't drink any more, I'm told. Or roam the streets. Your new girlfriend put her foot down. Dulcie; sweet by name and sweet by nature, I'm sure. Gets you in bed before daylight, I hear; she must be good for you. Pretty. Feminine. Petite. Goes to a good hairdresser too, I'd say. Must go out of town because she doesn't come to me. You've done well, finding such a girl to stay home for. She must be a calming influence. Pity she can't dance.

You are watching the dancers. Your attention is taken by one couple and then another – those feet, hips, that clinch. I watch your eyes cast across the floor, slowly, studiously. When, finally, you look in my direction, I can return your gaze for only the briefest moment. Consider yourself kissed.

A Natural Condition

WHITE POLKA DOTS on a red background with a daft wee frill at the hips; the swimsuit made her look like an Easter egg with tap roots. At least the sauna was quiet; just her and another woman who stared blatantly as she hoisted herself on to the slatted bench, eased her back against the blistering walls and attempted to relax.

Even under the forgiving red bulb, the veins on her chest and thighs stood out, thick and blue and throbbing. Not a pretty sight. But she was out of the rain, away from the leaden sky and the perpetual drumming on the roof. Every morning she prayed for a dry day so she could escape the salmon-pink walls of the apartment which, like the smell of fish and numerous other unpredictable odours, turned her stomach.

It had been raining for weeks without stopping, the same relentless downpour day after day, night after night. The rain was responsible for preserving areas of virgin forest but God was it monotonous. The leisure centre wouldn't have been her choice but it was there or the mall and anywhere was better than the mall with its muzak, its drift of mesmerised trolley pushers and clots of bored teenagers, consoling themselves with milk shakes and jumbo cartons of French fries.

—That's a wild swimsuit.

—It belongs to a friend. She's finished having babies.

—Lucky friend.

The woman tipped a ladleful of mentholated water on the coals; the temperature soared.

—Your first?

—Uh-huh.

—You sure ain't got long to go.

—Two weeks.

—Everything drags near the due date. I remember that all right. But believe me, you've got the easy bit right now; just you sit back and enjoy every single moment. These are your last two weeks of freedom. You wanna treat yourself like a queen because two weeks from now you're gonna wake up and find you're a slave. Still, you shouldn't be in here, honey. Too hot. Sauna's off-limits to pregnant women and folks with heart conditions. Used to be a sign but some kids was fooling with it, mixing up the letters and drawing dirty pictures. Management took it down for cleaning and didn't get around to putting it back up. But that's what it said and I sure don't want no emergencies in here. This place is for relaxation. I got enough stress waiting for me outside that door.

The woman adjusted her tiny turquoise bikini and spread herself over the bench. She was broad and smooth and brown, like polished maple.

—Why don't you try the kiddies' pool? It's warm enough just to lay around.

It was more of a command than a suggestion.

No aqua-fit – the perky grannies bobbing about in the shallow end and pumping tanned, sinewy arms like propaganda for a totalitarian state had defeated her – and now no sauna. She hadn't asked about saunas, hadn't asked much about anything. According to the doctor, a silver-haired Welshman with crinkly eyes and a non-intrusive approach to health, pregnancy was a natural condition and nothing to worry about. She worried all the same, slept badly and didn't feel natural at all; she felt invaded, occupied.

Beneath a garish, nursery-style mural of unlikely chickens and rabbits, she shouldered up against a water jet, gripped the rail with her hands and let her feet float to the surface. The jet rippled down her backbone like firm, trained fingertips and the water's buoyancy was a welcome change from dragging about, clumsy but fragile. The contradictions were maddening; to be ravenous and queasy at the same time, wide awake and exhausted; the body didn't seem like a very well-designed system. And this was just the beginning; she could think no further than the birth.

Dotted around the small, shallow pool, mothers patiently dandled their slithery wee bundles, echoing every chortle and squeal, applauding every involuntary gesture. All that maternal bonding. Did it happen automatically, or was it something you had to work at? And what if it didn't happen, what if she didn't bond with the baby, if she didn't like it, or it didn't like her?

Before the rainy season began, Liz – the original owner of the swimsuit – and her three pre-school kids, had persuaded her to accompany them to a petting farm where rabbits, goats and other cute furry animals were on hand to be fed, patted and cooed over. It had been fine until Liz's youngest, Amy, had dragged her into the hot, bright hatchery, which smelled of feathers, sawdust and chickenshit. It had made her dizzy but she couldn't leave because the child – an angel-haired cherub with a hot, determined grip – had dragged her towards the incubator to witness an egg cracking open. Another recently hatched chick was assisting from the outside by pecking at the shell – out of greed rather than altruism – there was albumen to eat. A stumbling ball of feathers and gristle burst out of the shell, unravelling itself. When the chick wobbled on to its splayed feet, soft, shivering and new, it looked far too big for its shell.

—Hey!

A big kid had dive-bombed into the kiddies' pool, splashing water everywhere and crashing against her legs. When he surfaced his eyes widened at the sight of the polka-dot bump protruding from the water. Grinning vaguely, he flopped on to his back and swished around until he'd positioned his head against the wall right beside her. A dripping lock of black hair fell across one eye. He was far too big to be in the kiddies' pool. Almost fully grown. Fourteen, fifteen, maybe. She could hear his breathing, thick and male, feel his breath on her cheek as he spoke.

—What is it?

He was eyeing the bump like some kind of poisonous toadstool. He must know. He must. Unless there was something wrong with him. This thought, like all worrying thoughts, transmitted itself intravenously to the baby who responded by delivering a sharp jab to her groin. She gasped and clutched at the bump. Maybe it was turning round, moving down, maybe the head was engaging. This imminent development had been bothering her for a while. What exactly was it meant to engage with and how would she know if it had done so? Was the locking sensation across her pelvis a real contraction or the trick kind, the Braxton Hicks, which could happen any old time and didn't mean a thing? It hurt but did it hurt enough?

The kid had slipped away from the side and was floating around her like a big stick of driftwood. He was too close, too bloody close. In her present condition, closeness was a problem, the nearness of strangers; crowds and people in a hurry were to be avoided. In a big country like this, one of vast empty spaces, where people habitually stood yards apart and yelled to each other across parking lots, there was no need to shove up against her like this, no need at all.

First a foot jutting out of the water, long twisted toes wiggling stiffly, and then the leg, waving around inches from her face. She couldn't help looking, couldn't help seeing the scar, white and lumpy, like a cable of melted plastic running from hip to knee. Nasty. And the kid was showing it off to her.

—Skate blade cut me up. Made front page in the local paper. Photo of Ma dragging me off the ice.

In response, the baby squirmed and kicked.

—There's Ma, right now, he said, pointing to the woman in the turquoise bikini, who was padding along to the changing rooms, ignoring her son's outlandishly waving foot.

—It's ladies' day for the sauna, he said. Always brings me on ladies' day so she can roast her butt in peace. So what d'you want; a boy or a girl?

—I don't mind.

—'Long as it's healthy, right?

—Right.

—'Long as it's got all its bits in the right place. First off, that's all anybody cares about but after a coupla years a kid's gotta be smart and good and cute too. Swimming's boring. But I don't play hockey no more.

—That's a shame.

—Yeah.

He plunged into the shallow water, swam to the steps, hauled himself out of the pool and limped to the showers, the spoiled leg trailing behind him.

The aqua-fit class had moved on to dry land and become a jiggling, poolside samba. Shrivelled, scrawny women, women inflated like inner tubes being tested for punctures, women who looked as if they'd been grafted together from mismatched pieces, all of them hopped and skipped and shook their stuff after their perfectly proportioned instructor. She closed her eyes and tried to concentrate on the relaxing effects of the water jet but there was too much noise, too much strenuous activity in the air.

By the time she negotiated the flimsy metal steps, steered her precarious bulk across slippery tiles and squeezed through the door to the changing room, the kid's mother was already dressed, in stressed red jeans and a black sweatshirt with the words *Jesus Saves But I Want Credit* printed on the back in dollar-bill green. She looked up from combing her long black hair.

—You sure ain't got long, honey. Look like you gonna bust right open.

She tried a smile but her mouth felt as overstretched as everything else.

—I just met your boy. In the kiddies' pool.

—Dumb kid. I keep tellin him to stay outa there. Them new moms don't like him hangin round their babies. They see that messed-up leg and start gettin the horrors. Right now, their cute little bundle of joy is safe in Mommy's arms. Nobody but nobody can harm a hair of its head while she's watchin but it can't last. Sooner or later some calamity's gonna happen . . .

—Must have been bad, the accident.

—Coulda been worse. Coulda been his face. Weird kid. Dunno where his head's at.

The woman secured her hair in a ponytail, frowned at her reflection and picked up her sports bag.

—Well, so long. Wish I knew where to get me a swimsuit like that.

Slowly she peeled off the polka-dots and began to dry herself. Everything had become an effort and the smallest effort was exhausting. Would she find the energy for labour? Tying her shoelaces was trouble enough.

The foyer of the sports complex was busy; flushed, shiny-eyed women sipped coffee and Cup-a-Soup from the vending machine and patted puffballs of blow-dried hair. Toddlers struggled as their mothers zipped them into rainsuits and tied the drawstrings on hoods, squashing their perfect faces into scowling pouts. As the lunchtime pool users prepared to leave, the afternoon hockey players were arriving, big dripping lads who congregated in a disaffected line against the far wall, skates slung heavily round their necks. Like trophies. Or yokes. She buttoned up her tent of a coat. The bus was due soon and she didn't want to miss it.

—Hi.

—Hello again.

—How're ya doin?

—OK . . .

—You know what? Ma's split. Just gone on home

without me. Does it all the time. Won't wait five minutes for me. Just walks straight out that door and don't look back. If the bus comes she gets on, even if I'm like running to catch up with her. Well, I ain't friggin running today . . . got something for you.

Glancing over at the skaters, he dug his hands into the pockets of his baggy parka and pulled out a hockey puck. He held it up close to her face and turned it round slowly. Embossed on the side, red letters on black, she read: NANAIMO V. HELSINKI: 1987.

—Belonged to my old man. He played in that game, in goal. His team lost. He didn't come home that night or any other friggin night. He lost a hockey game and me . . . ? Take it. Make a good paperweight. Or give it to the baby when it's bigger. Whatever.

—You should . . . shouldn't you . . . keep it?

—For what?

—I don't know, just in case.

—In case what? In case my old man shows up? I want you to have it, right. I want to give it to you . . .

He was pressing the puck into her hands and she was pushing it back towards him as, from across the foyer, guffaws spluttered from voices recently broken and others trying hard to break. A Coke can, kicked across the floor, skidded to a halt between the two of them and rattled feebly. Pain crunched into her pelvis like a nutcracker.

—You OK?

—I'll be OK in a minute.

—You don't look OK. You look sick.

—No . . . no, this is a . . . natural condition.

A bell rang and the hockey players – all awkward arms

and big feet – stomped towards the entrance to the ice rink, shoulders hunched under the weight of their skates. Another crushed drinks can clattered towards them.

—Go for it, Crow!

—Yeah, go for it, Crow. Score!

—What you been up to, Crow?

—Who's he been up?

—Crow don't do that stuff. Crow don't know how.

—Sure he does. Crow's done a whole bunch of training in that area. Trouble is, he likes to keep it in the family. Crow's a mommy's boy. Am I right, or am I right?

The kid barely seemed to hear their taunts. He was rigid, eyes fixed on the floor-to-ceiling window. In the distance, through the steamed-up glass, the blurred shape of a woman was visible, a woman in red and black, ponytail swinging defiantly as she hurried up the path and climbed on to a waiting bus. With a cry like ice cracking, he raised his arm and lobbed the puck at the window. He couldn't miss.

and big feet stamped towards the entrance to the [illegible] tank shoulder, hunched under the weight of their [illegible] Another [illegible] [illegible] towards them.

—Go for it, now.

—[illegible] go to [illegible], Sergei.

—What you [illegible] us to, [illegible]

—Who is he [illegible]

—[illegible] that stuff ... we don't have now.

—[illegible] a whole [illegible] [illegible] [illegible] the [illegible] the family [illegible] right.

The [illegible] [illegible] the [illegible] window [illegible] the [illegible] woman [illegible] [illegible] raised his [illegible] and [illegible] the [illegible] the window. The [illegible]

A Living Legend

LISTEN, IT MUST be almost a full house; can you hear the deep rumble, the unspoken communion of strangers, of people who've paid good money and come out on a bitter stormy night to hear *A Living Legend?* This is how Clem bills Belle on the posters. What he called her when she locked him out of the dressing room tonight was not so grand. Belle yelled back something even worse through the closed door. I laughed – quietly – and swept up the remains of the broken glass before she could do herself, or me, any damage.

Belle doesn't like my trilling, nervous laughs. Nor Clem's chewed, sour snorts. The only sounds which please her are the whoops of a full house. Don't you think it's odd, really, when Belle is in the business of tears? I have never been able to understand how it can be good to feel bad but that's what her audience pays for, every time. When Belle sings cheerful songs people shift in their seats and clear their throats. It's sadness which makes hundreds – of course it used to be thousands – hold their breath as one, the sadness of this difficult, contrary old woman who can barely remember her own words and may have trouble staying on her feet.

Belle's sadness is not a stage act, turned on to please the crowd, no, it is real and has been so right from the beginning, sadness she couldn't disguise even if she wanted to. In every photo, every film clip, even when her mouth is stretched into a wide glittering smile, her eyes shine with tears. And anger, too. Belle's sadness and her anger know no limits. They have accompanied her around the world, her invisible baggage, her demons, the blue moods and the black.

It took the entire journey here for Clem to persuade her not to cancel; Belle yelling, Clem slapping the steering wheel, the van roaring up the motorway at I don't know what speed. I prayed for deliverance and looked out of the window at ribbed brown fields and fat factory chimneys, at more fields, bridges and a long steel-grey curl of coastline. These dogfights must be endured, they are part of the job, but to be trapped in a van smelling of cigarettes and too many years on the road, hearing Belle and Clem pound each other with words blunt and heavy as bricks – it makes me shrink inside. Though I believe that everything is ordained, it is not good to be enclosed in a speeding capsule of rage.

In a way it is a good thing to see a piano on stage. Belle can lean against it for a song or two. Otherwise, by about halfway through the set, she might begin to totter a little. The audience might not notice but Clem, later, will curse her every unrehearsed step and fluffed songline. He will scold her like the unloved child she has always felt herself to be. She will purse her lips, scowl and possibly break something else. Clem says he would prefer an impersonator to the real Belle. An impersonator, Clem says, could do a better job of being Belle than Belle can now make of herself.

The bad thing about a piano being available is that Belle still has the unfortunate desire to play. I can see it in her eyes when she goes on stage, that invisible thread, pulling. Belle loves the piano better than any of the men who have passed through her life and are now no more than half-forgotten lyrics. The piano has been her solace, her confidante; the white in Paris, black lacquer in Tokyo, the walnut in Rome. But now, in her hour of need, the piano, too, betrays her. I expect you are wondering why I use such a gloomy word as betrayal. An old-fashioned word, and an old-fashioned idea. But Belle also talks about betrayal; by lovers and managers and recording companies. When she is allowed to. She is under contract not to speak about any of these things in public but, as you might expect, Belle has little respect for contracts. Contracts have cheated her too many times, kept her in her cage of pain. But she has lived like this so long, captivity is what she knows and, like a bird hurling itself against the bars, Belle bruises herself more than anybody else.

Tonight's venue is a church, at least it used to be a church; now it's a concert hall. It's fresh and bright, not at all the kind of place to which Belle has become accustomed. Most of the audience sit in hard, high-backed pews. The rest – who paid more for their tickets – cluster round candlelit tables in front of the stage. Drinks can be brought through from the bar so people can pretend that they're in a nightclub even though the ceiling is arched like a Gothic heaven and smoking is forbidden. A proper nightclub would have been more appropriate. I don't like the sham of the place though the dressing rooms are clean, chilly but clean. Belle likes the venue, the churchy feel. Uplifting, she says, and the acoustics are good. Maybe, but the PA system's so fuzzy that the acoustics hardly matter. And the band – I am not musical but even I know when a rhythm guitarist can't keep time.

Belle should not be blamed for the band. Clem hired

the musicians and Clem cares more about cost than quality. He must have scraped the scrapings for this lot. Clem says Belle is lucky to get any kind of band at all with her reputation. I don't deny that she can be difficult. I know as well as anyone just how difficult she can be. But we were not put on this earth perfect, our purpose is to grow towards perfection, however long it may take. Belle believes this too and knows it may take more time than she has left to reach a state of grace.

I do not talk to Belle of faith. It is she who talks of such things. The further she strays, the more she talks about needing to get back to the fold. It is never too late, I tell her, but Belle is scared of her sins, scared to look them in the eye, to name them. It breaks my heart every time I see her turn to the mirror, stare into her own sad black eyes, clip on big, shiny earrings, slick her mouth with lipstick then unlock the box where she keeps her needles and powders, the only comfort Clem has ever provided. It breaks my heart because, for Belle, happiness is no more than relief from pain.

The house lights are down and from the stage, Belle is looking out on a swaying sea of flames. Maybe the candles will help her forget Clem's threat that this may be the last night of the last ever tour, that if she screws up one more time, or blabs about business, she'll never see the inside of another dressing room, never mind step on to a stage. Clem has said this before, countless times, but this time I think he means it. Clem has plans for the future which don't include Belle. Lately, he has been doing a lot of talking on the phone; he is hunting down a new name, a new girl to groom for fame, a new voice to pour its heart out for a miserly percentage. If the deal goes through, Clem will have no more need for Belle.

Earlier tonight I had to stand in for her because she wouldn't do a lighting test. Clem had been rude to her and, of course, she was rude back. Belle has never been a good friend to herself, which is why I stay by her side, even when she hates the sight of me and curses me for shadowing her like the devil's own disciple. I know why Belle hits out at me; this, I understand. Other things are beyond me, but it is not for me to question what I don't understand. I do what must be done and so I walked around the stage, stopping where I was told, watching as a cool, serene space put on its red dress and pretended to become a nightclub.

Belle is wearing indigo. It's a soothing colour, indigo, deep and dark as the night sky but Clem doesn't like it, says it's too heavy, too ethnic; he wants her to shimmer in champagne silk and oyster satin, wants to put the Living Legend on stage, not the crazy old woman in an African wrap, with sharks' teeth round her neck and demons in her head. But Belle will not be told what to do or what to say; she has always been a woman with a will of her own. And a mouth as big as the Mississippi, says Belle. Which is true, and why Clem sits in the wings, head back, eyes closed, still as a dead man, listening hard, missing nothing.

Belle has been warned often enough that some things are OK to say out loud; others she must try to keep to herself. If she wants to talk politics, the history of oppression, black pride, the blues, she can go right ahead. She can talk about race and colour, poverty and inequality, conspiracy and murder. She can talk about Brother Malcolm's vision blurred and soiled by treachery. When she talks about Brother Malcolm, her eyes always search the darkness for me. It was he who brought us together all those years ago, who gave us each other. She can talk about her own attempts to embrace the Nation of Islam, and her failure to find redemption in faith.

Belle is free to talk about anything but business. She can complain all she wants about the injustices of the world as long as she doesn't mention the injustices of her own life. Clem will not tolerate this. He will hold it against her; on this he will not be crossed. As he sees it, Belle belongs to him because nobody else wants the trouble of trailing a has-been round provincial venues. Clem no longer cares for Belle and she has never cared for herself. All I can do is tend her wounds; I cannot cure the disease.

Tonight, the crowd is on her side, easy and kind, cheering wildly at every opportunity, hanging on every word, thrilled to be in her presence, no matter that the musical arrangements are harsh and ragged, that Belle's voice lost its wings long ago, its dip and soar, its ability to hover on a high note long enough to reduce a house to tears. This is a crowd which is trying hard to believe in the beauty behind a cracked voice and a band which sounds like the garbage being taken out, a crowd which strains to hear traces of Belle at her best and makes allowances for everything. These people want to cherish this shoddy performance, to take home personal memories of their idol, to talk years from now about the night they saw, in person, a Living Legend.

If only Belle could lose her need to gaze into darkness and flames; if she could take pleasure in other things – daylight, for example, birdsong, spots of sunlight marking out her kitchen floor. It is not my place to suggest this. It is only my place to be by her side when she needs me and absent when she needs to be alone, to stand in the wings while applause and the storm compete in rattling the roof of this deconsecrated place. Belle takes another bow and another. When the storm overwhelms the applause, she steps down from the stage, takes the glass of rye from me and the cigarette I have already lit for her. I offer her my arm. Wearily, we pick our way through darkness towards the glowing buzzer on the dressing-room door. Nearly there, I say, nearly there.

about when she needs to be alone [illegible] up in the [illegible]
[illegible] and [illegible] of
[illegible] Bell [illegible]
[illegible] her [illegible], she
[illegible]
and the [illegible]
[illegible] towards
[illegible] door. Near
[illegible]

Why Do the Hands Not Weep?

THE COFFEE WAS tepid, tarry and had probably been sitting on the hotplate since lunchtime but judging by the barmaid's blatant lack of interest in what little custom she had, the visitor reckoned that the odds on a fresh pot of coffee being brewed specially for her were about the same as being mistaken for a local. The barmaid wore the hotel uniform – tummy-hugging tartan skirt, matching waistcoat, white blouse with a flounce at the throat – emphasising the bossy chest and broad, childbearing hips which appeared to be native to the area. Had there been any other local women in the hotel bar of this small coastal town, other similarities might have been observed. No woman over thirty, for example, wore her hair past her shoulders and the repertoire of the town hairdresser ran to three styles: short bob, short perm and unisex crop. In clothing, lack of choice was also apparent: chunky, bum-concealing pink and peach jerkins had clearly been this season's job lot. Even lipstick shades remained smudged within the pink-to-peachy range.

Apart from the barmaid and herself, there were no women present. These were details which had caught the visitor's attention earlier in the day, as she'd walked back and forward along the curving promenade of the sturdy wee place, pausing at the playing fields like everybody else, to watch marquees being erected and Portaloos hoisted off a massive, articulated lorry and deposited behind a row of copper-berried rowans.

It was six o'clock and the townswomen would be at home, dishing out dinner to their families and discussing whether the weather would settle down and behave itself for the next day. A sudden downpour had made the visitor take shelter in the hotel bar – there was nowhere else nearby except the seaman's mission which was closed in preparation for the event of the summer, the Games. Nobody called them the Highland Games except outsiders, like herself, who came up from the south to watch the quaint but unsettling spectacle of burly men in kilts, whirling like pumped-up dervishes and tossing large heavy objects as far as momentum and meaty shoulders permitted.

The bar was a wilderness of floral carpeting and forlorn clusters of empty tables and chairs. One wall was given over to a plaster relief mural, a Scotch broth of things marine. A handsome, jolly fisherman, the centrepiece of the composition, was as close to the real thing as a battered haddock is to what swims in the sea. A sample of the real thing sat round the only other occupied table. Three men, straight from work, an old boy, a middle-aged one and a chubby-cheeked lad, were putting away a few pints before wending their way home. Their clothes were larded with oil, fish scales, blood and other unidentifiable clart. From where the visitor was sitting, she could smell fish guts and sweat. A pale haze of cigarette smoke rose from the centre of the table and curled round the men, containing and defining them, binding them together in their common purpose.

The old boy with the raw cheeks, watery eyes and chewed-looking woolly hat was grinning at her, his mouth forming an inaudible invitation. He held up his whisky, as if he were proposing a toast and, with his free hand, beckoned her over. She smiled and shook her head.

—D'you do reflexology? the young one asked her.

—No. Why?

—You look like you'd do reflexology. The hippy gear and that. I've done ma back in.

—Well, bed's the best place for you.

She realised her gaff too late; nudges and sniggers rippled round the table.

—Come on over, Blondie. Ye look that lonely there.

—I'm fine.

—We'll no bite.

—Unless ye ask nicely.

The barmaid, who'd heard every word though her gaze had been trained on the door, had a weak chin, a shelving mouth and the cold fathomless glare of a shark. She served her customers because that was her job. She was under no obligation to be pleasant to them and the idea of encouraging custom by hospitable chit-chat was clearly a foreign and therefore dubious notion. Even her regulars were there on sufferance.

The visitor sipped her disgusting coffee and looked out of the window. The rain had stopped as suddenly as it had started. Grey sky had given way to a thin, watery yellow. Clouds, in glittering shades of pewter and lilac, floated above the bay like big slow fish. The sun came out from behind a shoal of herring-coloured chevrons and dazzled her. It didn't surprise her that a lone woman – and a visitor at that – was still considered fair game, but she wasn't in the mood for drunks. She'd leave shortly and drive the hellish but spectacular road back to the B & B, to her small pink room with its brushed-nylon bed sheets and a box of Bibles in the wardrobe.

—I've come to talk to you.

The middle-aged one dumped his pint glass on the table and sat down. He must have been in his early fifties, though his peat-brown hair was thick and springy with no trace of grey. His crumpled shirt, open at the neck, revealed a small St Christopher on a thick, gold chain.

—I'm a rich man, he said. I don't want for anything. See that, he said, pointing to the fish-packing warehouse on the dock, that's mine. See that car – that silver Mercedes – that's mine too. I've done fine for myself.

He belched, apologised and downed a couple more inches of his pint.

—D'you mind me talking to you? I'm not wanting to be a bother.

Not feeling up to brutal honesty, she smiled and said nothing.

—Are you here for the games?

—Not specially but as they're on . . .

—I'll not be going. The whole town will be there but not me.

His name, he told her, was Kurt. A Dutchman, he'd worked his way round the ports of Britain and settled in this quiet wee place with its glorious light, grand mountains and sheltered bays.

—Are ye no bringin Blondie over here? said the young one with the bad back. You're no the only one who likes a bit fresh company, man.

—Wheesht, the old boy slurred. Let him be.

—Nae much crack in Kurt, Blondie. Ah could entertain ye better'n that auld misery.

The old boy grasped the young one's drinking arm and leaned forward until their faces were almost touching.

—You'd be doing everybody a good turn, laddie, including yourself, if you'd keep that big stupid gob of yours shut.

Unaware of the conversation at the other table, or choosing to ignore it, Kurt gripped the edge of the table, rocking forward and breathing his beery breath into her face.

—I won't go to the games.

—Yes, you said that.

—Did I? Aye, Blondie. I say things over and over. The lads there, they're sick of listening to me.

—Everybody repeats themselves when they're drunk.

—Drunk? I'm not drunk . . . yet. Can I talk to you?

—You *are* talking to me.

—Ach . . .

Kurt turned away and cast his eyes over the empty bar. The shark-faced barmaid was leaning against the till, worrying the flounce on her blouse.

—See her there? said Kurt. My sister-in-law. A yak-yak. She'll tell my wife I was talking to you. Troublemaker. Fuckin yak-yak.

His hands were flattened against the varnished wood. A gleaming wedding band hooped a chapped finger.

—I'll buy you a drink.

—I don't want a drink.

—I've plenty money. I'm a rich man. I want for nothing.

—A Coke then. I'm driving.

—Hah! Driving! Me too.

—You know the roads.

—Aye, Blondie, I know the roads, like the back of my hands.

Kurt splayed his fingers as wide as they would go, till the veins stood out like a network of converging paths or streams. Through the thin, almost transparent skin, the blue-green tributaries jumped and throbbed. She could almost see the blood pulsing through them. At the knuckles, the slack rucked into little wrinkled mouths but Kurt wasn't seeing his hands, the table they pressed against, the floral carpet.

—I've put new brake pads in my car, he said.

He stood up abruptly and went to the bar. His sister-in-law unfolded her arms and, without a word to him, pulled three pints and lined them up.

—And a Coke was it, for your . . . *friend*?

The final word rang out, cold and shrill, its meaning rubbished by the intonation, the implication.

—Aye.

—Would she be wanting ice with that?

—Aye. And a slice of lemon and all, if it's not too much trouble for you.

Kurt and his sister-in-law exchanged cash for goods without the aid of any social pleasantries.

The visitor realised too late that she should have gone after her coffee and avoided being drawn into this inbred, insular animosity. She'd come for the light, the space, for the absence of noise, dirt, too many people and too much to do. She'd come to watch the changing colours of sea, sky and land. Seven hours driving it had taken to get here, to get away from her own insular domestic bickering. Why waste precious time on somebody else's?

—I don't believe in life after death, says Kurt. Do you?

—No.

—When you're dead you're dead. And that's it.

—That's what I think. But nobody can know for certain.

—So I'm never going to see my boy again, am I, Blondie?

That was when he began to talk, the man with the lucrative fish business and the silver Mercedes, when he began to tell the visitor his story of last year's games, the big turnout, the disappointing weather, the beer tent awash with drenched bodies, the humiliation of incomers scooping the lion's share of the prizes. But in spite of the weather and cultural pride being undermined, a good do. A family get-together too, their eldest boy home for the games, grown-up now, independent, with steady work not too far south. Always a close family, a tight crew, their lives lashed together, part of the same mesh. And after the Games, the Ceilidh; the games weren't the same without the ceilidh after. Everybody spruced up, the men smelling of pine, the women sweet as clover, half-bottles in hip pockets, a flame in every heart as the fiddlers tuned up, the grime and grind of work washed away as the dancers took their partners. The hours just birled away.

Of course some always drew the short straw. Folk had to get home somehow and what did you do if there were no buses, trains or taxis? Not his own boy driving but a school friend – just qualified as an engineer – who'd sensibly stuck to LA lager, orange squash and stewed tea. It could have been drink, drink took so many on the roads and off them. It could have been drink but it was a stag, hot on the heels of a hind, leaping blindly into the road, smashing into the windscreen. Four boys dead, the stag too, just before dawn on the coast road south.

* * *

—The wife won't stop crying. Folk from the church keep coming to the house and saying: God loves us, our boy is alive in our hearts . . . but when you're dead, you're dead, Blondie. And that's it . . . D'you mind me talking to you? The lads there, they don't hear me any more.

She looks out of the window. In the rain-washed evening light, the shingle glitters. Along the curve of the bay, draped between street lights, multicoloured bunting flaps softly. People are out walking, locals in pastel jerkins, visitors in slime-coloured Barbours. She can see her car, parked near the war memorial. A stone soldier, gun in hand, searches the bay for enemies. An irreverent gull perches on his head. Beyond the purled, treacherous road, the setting sun has gilded the peaks of Assynt: Ben Glas, Canisp, Cul Mor, Stac Pollaidh, Suilven. Could there be anything more like heaven on earth than the light on those ancient, unique peaks? It's said that God was practising when he threw those lumps of rock at the land, one by one, like a novice potter chucking clay at a spinning wheel, hoping to hit centre. One-off mountains, mountains to fall down and worship, not for their perfection but their endurance, mountains to love because they are there, have been and will be long before and long after everything imaginable . . .

. . . But a mountain does not speak the same language, sky can't share joy, hope, sorrow. Does sorrow only reveal itself through the eyes? What of the hands, which have held the loved, lost one, why do the hands not weep?

Kurt's fingers are laced together like a cradle, or a net in which he has landed too heavy a catch.